WHAT LIES WITHIN

JAMIE CORTLAND

This is a work of fiction. Names, characters, places, and incidents are products of the author's imagination or are used fictitiously and are not to be construed as real. Any resemblance to actual events, locations, organizations, or person, living or dead, is entirely coincidental.

WCP

World Castle Publishing, LLC
Pensacola, Florida

Copyright © Jamie Cortland 2014
Print ISBN: 9781629891767
eBook ISBN: 9781629891774
World Castle Publishing, LLC, December 15, 2014
http://www.worldcastlepublishing.com

Licensing Notes

Cover: Karen Fuller
Editor: Brieanna Robertson

Previously published under the title of "Skin Deep" this novel has been revised and re-edited, and re-titled by the author.

CHAPTER 1

She closed her eyes and drifted off, dreaming of a perfect stranger. The man in her dream was tall, handsome, and slender with blue-green eyes and dark, wavy hair. He was a widower in his mid-thirties, wealthy, and able to travel. When he reached out to touch her, his touch seared her; his face grew distorted. Evelyn screamed. Sitting straight up in bed, she stared into darkness. Reaching over to the brass lamp that sat on the end table, she turned it on.

"Mommy, Mommy!" The door flung open and Chrissie ran in and jumped on her bed. "Are you all right? I thought I heard you scream."

"I had a nightmare. I'm all right, Chrissie. Go back to bed."

"Can I sleep with you? I'll protect you, Mommy."

Evelyn chuckled. "All right, dear. We'll go to breakfast in the morning. Would you like that?"

"Yes. Let's do that. Can I order some of those pancakes I like, with the strawberries and whipped cream?" she asked, snuggling under the covers.

"Of course. Now, go back to sleep. I promise I won't have any more nightmares."

"Okay. But, Mommy, did you dream of monsters?"

"Sort of."

"That's scary. We need a doggie to protect us. Can we get one? Please?"

A light knock came at the door and then it opened a crack.

"Mom?"

"Are you all right, Evelyn? I thought I heard you scream."

"Come in, Mom. Chrissie heard me too. She crawled in bed with me to keep me safe."

"You're a brave little girl, Chrissie," Katherine said.

"Mmm. Hmm. Grandma, could we have a doggie?"

Katherine glanced at Evelyn. "We'll talk about that later, dear. We'll need to ask Grandpa."

"Oh goodie. I know he'll say yes."

"If everything's all right, I think I'll go back to bed," Katherine said.

"Can I still stay here with you, Mommy?"

The corners of Evelyn's mouth turned up in amusement. "Yes, dear. Just snuggle up under the covers and go back to sleep."

Evelyn reached up and turned off the light. The dream still lingered within her mind. What could it have meant? The stranger had been so handsome, nearly her ideal man until his face transformed into a monster's. She tried to shrug it off and blame it on her favorite TV show and the chocolate ice cream she'd eaten before she'd gone to bed.

Closing her eyes, her thoughts turned to Thomas. She wished with all her heart that he hadn't betrayed her. Night after night, she slept in their bed alone. Since their divorce, she had missed him terribly. Perhaps she should have given him more of a chance to explain his side, but she'd been furious about his obvious betrayal. His feeble explanations had fallen on deaf ears.

Other than missing him, she was perfectly happy. She loved her career, lived in a wonderful loving home with her darling three-year-old daughter Chrissie and her parents. Set on two and a half acres, the four-bedroom, four-bath Spanish-style home in Paradise Valley, Arizona offered a large Olympic-sized pool, a Jacuzzi, and tennis courts. They were not at all crowded. The only thing in her life she lacked was a man who loved her, someone that she could love and respect who would accept Chrissie.

Thomas had not given up. He still believed she would come back to him, that she would realize it had just been gossip, that he had been faithful to her. She would never believe it. The evidence was too obvious. She'd been humiliated in public, and the pain of his betrayal still haunted her. Thomas was famous, not only for his wonderful singing voice, but also for the films he had recently starred in. It was said that he'd been having an affair with his agent, one that had become scandalous. He was a public figure after all…a superstar. If she lived to be a hundred and one, she never wanted to be with anyone famous again. Not even almost famous.

CHAPTER 2

James tossed and turned. In his dream, he lived a nightmare of the past. He tried to block out the scene that played on the canvas of his dream, but the images would not disappear, nor would the voices.

"Go then and good riddance." Brakes screeched as a fire-engine-red Pontiac raced over the bridge and struck Elaine. Her shrill scream cut through the early evening hours. Thump! Thump! *She flew up onto the hood of the car, bounced twice, and landed hard onto the pavement. Traffic on Palmetto Park Road backed up for miles as she lay dying just across the street from her favorite restaurant. Blood oozed from her head and puddled onto the hot asphalt.*

James sat straight up in bed. Perspiration beaded on his forehead. Screams echoed in his mind along with a vision of his wife dying just a few feet away from him. He'd had this dream every night on the anniversary of Elaine's death for the past twelve years. Had he pushed her? He might have wanted to, but in his right mind, he would never have killed anyone. Even though he'd never been baptized, he'd been brought up Christian. By the time he was six years old, he knew the Ten Commandments.

Though the fatal accident had happened years ago, the day still remained crystal clear in his mind. When he'd awakened that morning, he'd gone for his usual morning beach walk. It was hot and humid, unbearably so even for six-thirty in the morning. That in itself was not unusual, not for Florida. The heavy rain-laden clouds and warm waters of the Atlantic promised a tropical storm was brewing. Lately, his mind had been as stormy as the weather forecast. He'd been hearing voices again, voices that drove him past the edge of sanity. When Elaine had been killed, Bobby had only been three years old. After that day, he'd raised his son alone. Perhaps Bobby had been better off without a mother, like the voices had said.

Elaine had been unfaithful to him for as long as he could remember. Steve had told him he'd seen Elaine in restaurants with men when he'd been out of town. Since Steve had been a friend of his mother's for most of her life, he had no reason to doubt him. When he'd accused Elaine, she'd denied it. She'd wanted a divorce, full custody of their son, alimony, child support, and their home. He'd desperately wanted her out of the way. Maybe he *had* pushed her. Was this Elaine's way of punishing him if he had? By haunting him?

His grandmother had once told him about earthbound spirits who could not or did not want to move on. Most were unfortunate souls who were lost or had been killed suddenly. Others were addicts, still craving their addictions, feeding off the living, particularly those who were alcoholics. She told him how lost spirits hovered over drinking establishments, waiting to possess an inebriated warm body. He didn't believe it. He didn't want to. He shuddered and tried to remember what had happened that evening, just like he did every year on the anniversary of Elaine's death.

He'd been drinking heavily during the week before her accident, trying his best to mask the voices he heard inside his mind, voices insisting Elaine was fooling around. He raked his fingers through his hair. He couldn't remember clearly, but he recalled they'd had a fight. After that, he'd blacked out.

What did it matter? She was dead. He was alive. He needed a wife. He was tired of rotating girlfriends who wanted money, fancy cars, and a big house. He needed someone to love, someone who would love him unconditionally.

He rose and moved into the bathroom, shrugged out of his black silk pajamas, and stepped into the oversized marble shower of the villa he was staying in. He turned the water on and adjusted it until it was steaming hot. Standing under the hot water, he thought about the villas and how to solve their sales problems. He and his partners had built eighteen luxury villas in Paradise Valley thinking they'd sell quickly. They'd kept one for themselves for their frequent visits to Arizona. They'd miscalculated the market. They hadn't sold well. This morning, after he'd had breakfast, he planned to have a talk with the sales person on duty.

After he showered and dressed, he set out for a popular nearby coffee shop. A petite woman with highlighted blonde hair caught his eye. Stepping out of a silver Jaguar, she walked around to the other side of the car and helped a little girl with long, curly, chestnut brown hair out. As they moved toward the restaurant, the child clung to the woman's shapely leg while she walked. The woman stopped, bent down to speak with the child, then took her hand and entered the restaurant.

When he entered the restaurant, he saw that there was a wait. She and the child were sitting on a long sofa near the front door. He left his name with the hostess and moved to sit near the woman. Maybe God had answered his prayers.

"Do you mind if I take this seat? There's a wait."

She turned and flashed him a wide smile, her dimples showing. Her hazel eyes twinkled as though she had a tempting secret she'd like to share. "No, of course not. Please sit down."

"Wonderful day, isn't it?"

She nodded. "Yes, except it's stifling. August in Phoenix isn't the most desirable place to be."

He chuckled. "No. But neither is south Florida, where I'm from. At least Arizona doesn't have hurricanes."

"Thank God. So, you're from Florida. Where?"

He glanced down at her left hand. No ring. *More than likely, she's single.*

"Boca Raton. I have a home on the Atlantic," James said.

She nodded. "My aunt lives up the coast from you."

"Where?"

"Vero Beach."

"Do you visit often?" James asked.

"Occasionally."

"Mama," the little girl said. "Daddy said not to talk to strangers. He might be an ass murderer!"

"Axe murderer, darling," the woman said, correcting her daughter. "I don't think so, dear."

"Mama, Daddy said you can't always tell by a person's looks," the little girl said with a worried expression on her face.

James laughed. "That's true. My name is James

McMann. My partners and I built Sunset Villas about four blocks from here."

"It's nice to meet you, James. I'm Evelyn Valentino, and this is my daughter, Chrissie."

Chrissie tightened her mouth and turned her back on him.

"Where are your manners, Chrissie?" Evelyn asked.

"Just because he told you his name doesn't make him a friend," Chrissie said. "He's still a stranger and I'm not talking to Mr. Stranger Danger. I'm going to tell Daddy," she said, crossing her arms and tilting her chin up.

"I'm sorry, Mr. McMann," Evelyn said with an apologetic note in her voice.

"Actually, Mr. Valentino has a point. He's trained his daughter well," James said, withdrawing two business cards from his suit pocket. "My card, Mrs. Valentino, and one for you too, Chrissie."

"It's Ms. Valentino, and I just happen to be in the market for a villa," Evelyn said with a bright smile.

Am I in luck or what? "In that case, perhaps you would like to stop by the villas after breakfast?"

"I'm sorry. I have an appointment this morning."

"Then why not meet me for breakfast tomorrow morning, same time, same place. I'll bring a brochure of the villas. If they are something that might interest you, we can ride over after breakfast," James said, hoping her schedule was free.

"I'd like that," Evelyn said.

"Great!" James said with a wide grin.

"Mama, they're calling our name. Our table's ready," Chrissie said. She stood and took her mother's hand.

"Excuse me, Mr. McMann. It's been nice talking to you," Evelyn said, rising.

"I'll look forward to seeing you tomorrow morning. Call me at the number on my card if something comes up and you can't make it."

"I will. Oh! I almost forgot." She took a business card from her handbag. "You don't have my number. Just in case you need to reschedule, you may want my card."

"Thank you," he said, glancing at the elegant script. "So, you're a writer?"

"I'm a freelance writer," Evelyn said with a note of pride in her voice.

"What do you write? Articles?"

She nodded. "I write articles for various magazines and a few for newspapers."

"Interesting. You'll have to tell me more about it sometime. I'd like to read some of your work. Perhaps you could do a feature about Sunset Villas and our corporation, JVS Builders?"

"Sounds more like an ad. You need a publicist, not a freelance writer."

He watched her as she moved away. She possessed the bearing of royalty. He'd bet his bottom dollar this woman was not a fortune seeker. More than likely, she had money of her own or she had sucked Mr. Valentino dry. She'd left him wanting to know more.

****

Evelyn awoke the following morning with a nagging feeling of hesitancy about meeting with James McMann this morning. It wasn't the villas. Yesterday afternoon, she'd driven by them. They seemed to be exactly what she wanted. Painted a cream color with red tile roofs, they were heavily landscaped with palm trees, bougainvillea, and cactus. She didn't know what a lease would run, but if she were looking to buy, she was fairly certain the price was out of her range. For the first time, she wished she hadn't refused Thomas's offer of a sizeable settlement.

As it was, she had refused to accept either a settlement or alimony. The only thing she received from Thomas was child support for Chrissie for the time she was in her custody.

She rubbed her temples with her fingers. What was it about James McCann that bothered her? He seemed familiar, but her daughter had dubbed the handsome builder Mr. Stranger Danger. Whether or not he was dangerous, she'd been attracted to him. She needed to know more about him, she decided, as she rose and padded into the bathroom to shower. Perhaps Thomas had overstressed the need for caution with strangers to Chrissie. At the time, she had approved. Neither of them wanted to lose their precious daughter to a pedophile or a kidnapper.

As a superstar's daughter, danger often lurked around the corner.

****

James rinsed his mouth with a strong mouthwash, making sure not a trace of alcohol remained on his breath. Maybe he shouldn't have had the early morning Bloody Mary. He splashed on his favorite aftershave and left the townhouse, determined to make a good impression upon the attractive writer.

He popped a Tic Tac into his mouth and drove the white Lexus SUV that belonged to JVS Builders into the parking lot of the restaurant. There wasn't a silver Jag in sight. Either she hadn't arrived yet, or she wasn't coming. He glanced at his watch. 10:00 a.m. He was precisely on time. Stepping out of the car, he wiped the perspiration from his forehead. *They say it's dry heat here. Damn, dry heat or not, it's unbearably hot in Arizona in the summertime.* He wasn't sure which was hotter, Florida or Arizona. Hot was hot. Waiting on the bench outside the restaurant would be impossible. He bought a newspaper and went inside.

"A table for two, please. I'm waiting for Evelyn Valentino. She's a striking, petite blonde. Would you show her to my table when she arrives?"

"Of course. Ms. Valentino is one of our frequent customers."

He didn't need to wait long. Five minutes later, he saw Evelyn enter the restaurant alone, without the annoying child. She wore a white skirt, an orange knit top with a gold necklace, and dangling earrings to match. The image she created was so attractive and sexy, he wasn't sure if he was going to be able to keep his hands to himself.

"Wouldn't you like to warm her bed?"

"What are you doing here, Steve?"

"You didn't think I'd miss this, did you, James?"

"Get lost, Steve."

James watched as Evelyn stopped to speak with a man she evidently knew. A streak of jealousy shot through him as she smiled warmly. She moved to the hostess and briefly spoke with her. She turned and her eyes met his. She waved and moved to his table. He wondered how well she knew the man she'd spoken with.

"Sorry, I'm just a bit late," Evelyn said.

"Only a little," he said, concealing his brief anger. He rose and pulled out the chair to seat her.

"Thank you, James," she said, looking up into his eyes with an appreciative smile.

"You're most welcome." His heart lifted. He could hardly be angry with her after seeing her sweet smile.

"Would you like coffee?" he asked, sitting back down in his chair.

"Definitely. I was a bit in a rush when I left home and haven't had a cup of coffee yet."

"Neither have I and I'm not at my best without it," he said, motioning the waitress over. After his brief chat with Steve, he needed either coffee or a shot of vodka. He shouldn't have been here this morning.

"Two coffees and orange juice for both of us, please."

"Thank you, sir. I'll be back soon to take your order."

"I'm glad you could make it this morning, Evelyn," James said.

"So am I. I drove through Sunset Villas yesterday, but didn't stop. They're attractive. Dad said JVS has a fine reputation."

"Thank you. We take pride in our work. I think you will like the villas." He couldn't let her slip away. He felt this was the woman for him. He was wealthy, and if she could come close to the price, he could easily pick up the difference without her knowledge.

"I'm looking forward to seeing them, but I doubt I can afford one."

"You might be surprised. What's your price range?"

"Up to three hundred and fifty thousand."

"We might be able to work something out. If you're financing, there are various options available."

"Maybe I should wait."

"If you're uncomfortable about purchasing a condo, perhaps you might consider a lease with option to buy," James said.

"That's a possibility."

"We don't often do that, but perhaps in your case, we could make an exception. Have you always lived in the

Phoenix area?" James asked, wanting to know more of her background for himself more than for business.

"No. I was born in Phoenix, but after I married, I moved to Vegas," Evelyn said.

"Las Vegas? You're former husband isn't the famous Thomas Valentino, is he?" he asked, half joking.

"Yes," Evelyn said, hoping he hadn't seen the gossip in the papers.

"I thought I'd seen your photo before," James said.

She nearly groaned aloud. "You probably saw it in the tabloids. Our divorce was so public...our lives, too. In spite of it, Thomas and I are still good friends."

"For your daughter's sake, that's fortunate."

"Are you married, Mr. McMann?" Evelyn asked. She hadn't seen a wedding band.

"No. I'm a widower," James said with a sigh.

"I'm so sorry. I didn't know. You're young to be a widower," Evelyn drew her brows together. She wondered how his wife had died.

"My wife was killed an accident," he said in a low voice, as though he had read her mind.

"Auto?"

"Yes. Actually, she was crossing the street," James said, not explaining further.

"You weren't with her, were you?" Evelyn asked, horrified.

He nodded and said, "I should have been able to save her or at least prevent her from running across the street. I can still see every detail in my mind."

"That must have been terrible. You don't blame yourself, do you?" She was almost sorry she'd asked if he'd ever been married. For heaven's sake, his personal life was none of her business, not yet anyway.

"It was horrible," James said, running his hand through his dark, wavy hair. "Sometimes, I still have nightmares about it. Do I blame myself? Sometimes, but I don't think there was anything I could have done."

"I can only imagine how you must feel," Evelyn said, wanting to change the subject. It was clear James was still disturbed about the accident.

"If you don't mind, I'd rather not talk about it."

"Of course not. Forgive me. I didn't mean to pry." She would try to be more careful from now on.

"You must have a lot of friends here," he said, changing the subject. He didn't want to think about the accident. Every time he did, a vision of Elaine as she lay bleeding on the pavement flashed into his mind along with a brief pang of guilt. From what seemed to be a long way off, he heard Evelyn's reply, jolting him back to the present.

"A few. I was away for a while and lost touch."

"But your family lives here," James said. "I'm sure you must have kept up with some of your friends."

"We didn't visit that often and when we did, we were busy with family. And you? I believe you said you were from Florida?" She wanted to know more about JVS Builders.

"I live in Highland Beach, just north of Boca Raton. I'm originally from Boston."

"You still have a slight Boston accent. How long have you been in Boca?"

"We moved to Boca when I was eleven."

"You're almost a native then."

"You could say that."

"Do your parents still live in Boca?"

"Both of my parents are dead," James said in a dull

voice.

Evelyn cringed. She shouldn't have asked, but how could she have known? Besides, he was from out of town and she wanted to know who she was dealing with. So far, she didn't know anything except that his wife had been killed and that his parents were deceased. "I'm sorry," she said quietly.

"Me too," James said, casting his eyes down.

"You are so young to have lost both of your parents," Evelyn said, feeling badly for him.

"May I take your order now?" the waitress asked.

"Do you know what you would like, Evelyn?" James asked, glancing up at her.

"Yes. I'd like a Spanish omelet, made with egg whites only. Oh! And extra salsa on the side," she said with a smile to the waitress.

He grinned. "You like your breakfast hot and spicy, I see."

She nodded.

"I'll have a Spanish omelet too," James said.

"Would you excuse me a moment, Mr. McMann?" Evelyn asked.

"Call me James, please. Of course I'll excuse you."

He was glad she'd chosen to take that time to go to the ladies room. He watched as she moved away. Wearing high-heeled white, strappy sandals, she swayed slightly. When she was out of sight, he pulled a small vodka bottle from his jacket and poured it into his glass of fresh orange juice. He wished the subject of Elaine hadn't come up. It had set off the voices in his mind again. The vodka would help to keep them at bay.

He liked Evelyn. She was genuine and unaffected. After having been married to Thomas Valentino, she must have met some famous people. She could have been a name-dropper, but she didn't seem to be. Odd, though, that her price range was as low as it was. That in itself told him she hadn't soaked Valentino with a high alimony payment.

When they finished breakfast, she insisted upon following him in her car to the villas. Clearly, she didn't feel comfortable with him yet. The salesman wasn't in, which in his mind was for the best. He didn't want him interrupting.

While he waited for Evelyn in the sales office, he pondered what he could do to make her feel more at ease with him. It was obvious by her questions that she didn't trust him. He hadn't liked the memories her questions had stirred. Still irritated, he clenched his jaw while he scanned the floor plans. They needed to sell or at least rent the larger unit. Priced at $500,000, she probably wouldn't be able to afford it. Maybe Sal and Vince would agree to a lease. The model had been for sale for over a year without a nibble. Even for an unattached villa, it was large. Most of their customers wanted the two-bedroom model with an office.

"James? Are you busy now? I'm sorry it took me so long. I got caught up in traffic,"

Evelyn said, walking into the office.

He turned and grinned. Her highlighted blonde hair was disheveled, her hazel eyes wide. She was obviously harried. "Sit down a minute," he said.

Evelyn sat in the chair facing James and placed her handbag on the floor next to the chair. "I should have left with you, but I'm going to Carefree later for a gift. There is a wonderful gallery there that is my favorite."

"I haven't been to Carefree. Do you suppose we might

go together, that is, after you've seen the models?"

"Yes, of course. I'll need to call mother later and let her know since Chrissie is with her this morning. In fact, if you like, maybe we could have lunch at The Horney Toad. It's unique to the area and entirely different from what you would see in Florida."

"I'd like that," he said, forgetting about his appointment. "I've been thinking about the floor plans and the one I believe would be best for you. Would you like to see that one?"

"If it's a two-bedroom with an office."

"Hmm. The one I had planned on showing you is a bit larger. It's a three-bedroom with an office and a family room."

She shook her head. "That would be too large."

"Well then, let's start off with a two-bedroom with an office. We have one available."

"Wonderful," she said, rising.

"We'll take the golf cart," he said, opening the door of the sales office for her.

Evelyn moved toward the cart while James walked ahead and waited by the side of the cart. Evelyn stepped up, tottered, and began to fall backwards. He caught her around the waist and placed her neatly in the seat.

"Thank you," she said, still burning from his touch. She turned to face him, her eyes meeting his amused blue-green ones. Her face warmed. "I don't know what happened. My foot slipped, I guess."

"Don't worry about it. I'm just glad I was here to catch you," he said with a wide grin.

As they toured the property, she noticed the spectacular pool with a gorgeous fountain spilling over red rocks. A Jacuzzi and tennis courts completed the amenities.

"What do you think of the property so far?" James asked, anxious to have a commitment. He could think of nothing more pleasant than having Evelyn living nearby. It would bring a smile to his face every morning he woke up in Arizona.

"The development is charming," Evelyn said. Not only did the property appeal to her, but so did James. She found her trust in him building. She was glad Chrissie had not come with her. When she had toured the attractive villa with its gorgeous views of the surrounding mountains, she knew she wanted it. "Oh! This is magnificent."

Pleased, the corners of his mouth turned up. She would live here, in one of these villas. He'd see to it.

"Did you have anything to do with the architecture?"

"A little, in regard to the views, the built-in desk, and bookcases in the office," James said modestly.

"As far as I am concerned, those are the features that make this condo really special," Evelyn said with admiration reflected in her voice.

"Thank you. Did you like the kitchen?"

"I don't cook much. Since I work at home, I like to go out for my meals."

He drew his brows together. *That won't work for me. She will need to stop writing and focus upon homemaking…maybe take a gourmet cooking class.* He wondered how Thomas Valentino had been able to handle having a wife that didn't cook. He had probably hired a cook, one that doubled as an upstairs maid. He smirked. He couldn't imagine that the superstar had been faithful. He'd seen him in a couple of films and on stage in Vegas. He brought himself back to the present and asked,

"Would you like to purchase the villa?"

"I doubt I can afford it. You mentioned a lease with option to purchase. I would consider that depending upon the terms."

"Hmm. This plan is one of our most popular, but I'll speak to my partners and see what we can do."

"I would really appreciate that."

"Let's go on back to the office and I'll give you a brochure of the property," James said, helping her back into the cart. On the way back to the office, he asked, "Are you living in an apartment now?"

"No. Chrissie and I have been living with my parents since my divorce."

"It might be time to consider giving them a break," he said.

"Maybe, although I really think they enjoy having us around."

"What about you? You can't have much privacy."

"They have a large home. There's plenty of room. Still, it would be nice to have a place of my own."

"How does your daughter feel about it?" James asked.

"She loves being around her grandparents." She glanced at her watch. "I really need to be going. Are you still interested in going to Carefree and to lunch with me?" Evelyn asked as they stopped in front of the office.

He glanced at his watch. His heavy brows knitted together. "I'm sorry. I'd love to, but I have an appointment. I'd almost forgotten about it. Rain check?"

"Of course."

"I'll give you a call after I speak with my partners," James said, not really sure if either Vince or Sal would approve of leasing the unit. He'd need to do some arm twisting.

"Thank you so much for everything," she said as James helped her down from the golf cart. "I'll look forward to hearing from you."

He watched from the window of the sales office as she drove off.

"Your girlfriend?" the salesman asked.

"No, Ed. I wish. You'll be here until six p.m., won't you?" James asked.

"Yes," Ed said. "Are you expecting the lady back today?"

"No. Not today. I have an appointment and I need to leave, but we need to go over a couple of things when I get back. Sell a villa while I'm gone. But not number nine," James said, making certain the villa Evelyn liked would still be available.

The salesman nodded. "Done."

James didn't want to go to the appointment, but he'd been having problems again and he couldn't afford not to be on his toes. He hated the side effects the medication caused, but maybe in time he wouldn't need to take it. They'd told him there was no cure, only treatment. He didn't believe them, but for now, the business couldn't suffer due to his problems and neither could his personal life.

After his appointment, he placed a call to Vince and asked about Evelyn possibly leasing the particular villa that she wanted. They had five others just like it for sale.

"So, who's the girl? Are you dating her?" Vince asked.

"Evelyn Valentino."

"Thomas Valentino's wife?"

"Ex-wife. She's gorgeous. I'm not dating her. Not yet, anyway, but I hope to. From what I've read in the magazines, he's still carrying a torch for her. That's tough competition," James said.

"Give her a discount, a big one. We can use a looker and a celeb on site," Vince said.

"I was hoping you would say that, but the celeb better not be on site often. What about Sal? How do you think he will feel about it?"

"I'll run it by him tonight and let you know tomorrow," Vince said. "If she's as attractive as you say, Sal will agree to your proposal."

The following afternoon, James called Evelyn to let her know his partners had agreed to offer her a lease with option to buy on the townhouse she was interested in.

"How much did you say it would be per month?" Evelyn asked.

"Fifteen-hundred, furnished." That would mean he would need to replace the furniture in the model. But, he figured, Thomas Valentino no doubt still had the house and furniture in Vegas.

She gasped. "You must be offering me a huge discount."

"A little. After all, it is summertime, a slow period for us," James said.

"Well, I would love to live in the villa and I can hardly refuse such an offer."

"Would you like to stop by in the morning to sign the lease?"

"I'm sorry, I won't be able to tomorrow morning," Evelyn said, disappointed.

"Well then, there's a restaurant I'd like to go to while I'm here. I've heard a lot about it. Perhaps, you would like to have dinner with me at Pinnacle Peak tonight. You could sign the lease then."

"I'd love to, but if you haven't been there, you may

not know there is a dress code. Wear jeans, a shirt, or even a tee, but no tie. If you wear one, they'll cut it off," she said with a chuckle.

"So I've heard. Both my partners lost theirs. Would eight p.m. be all right? I'll pick you up," James said.

"I'll look forward to it. I'm sure Mom and Dad won't mind keeping Chrissie."

"If there's a problem, let me know." As much as he wanted to have dinner with Evelyn, he didn't want Evelyn's irritating child to go along with them.

"I will. As long as you're drawing up the lease, would it be all right if we start the first of the month?" Evelyn asked.

"No problem."

"Thanks very much. I'll see you tonight."

"Oops. I need the address of your parents' home, maybe directions, too," James said.

"Sorry," she said, and gave him the address and directions to their home.

After they'd hung up, James smiled. He was glad he hadn't been over anxious, easily available. He'd lied. He was free tomorrow morning, but he wanted to see her tonight, wanted to see where her parents lived and what her father did for a living.

****

Evelyn sucked in her breath when she opened the front door. Tall with wavy dark hair, blue-green eyes, and skin the color of polished almond, James looked devastatingly handsome in his blue and black plaid western shirt, black jeans, and black lizard boots. Topping it off, he wore a black western hat.

"Good evening, James," she said with a wide smile. "They'll be no cutting of ties for you this evening. If I didn't know you were from Florida, I'd say you look just like a long, tall Texan."

"Thanks, I think. You're looking wonderful. You should wear jeans more often," he said with an observant glance at her slim figure.

"Well, thank you. Come on in. I would like you to meet my parents."

He followed her into the living room. Warm and inviting, the ceilings were high with vigas, typical of Spanish architecture. A large kiva-style fireplace surrounded with blue and white mosaic tiles contained a huge Mexican clay pot filled with orange poppies that lent a cheeriness to the room. Beautiful western landscapes, seascapes of the Pacific, and a few North American Indian paintings decorated walls that shone golden in the sunlight yet peach in the shadowed areas. The furniture was eclectic, a perfect combination of antiques and Spanish style furniture.

After going through the formalities of introducing James to her parents, she stepped back, observing their reactions.

"It's nice to meet both of you," he said, shaking Dr. William O'Malley's hand. Moving to Katherine, he shook her hand. "Your home is quite attractive."

"Thank you. It's very comfortable and I loved decorating it," Katherine said.

"She's an excellent decorator, isn't she?" Dr. O'Malley asked proudly.

"I've not seen better," James said, meaning it.

"Well, you certainly know the right thing to say." Katherine's delight shone in her hazel eyes.

"I've heard a lot about you and your villas from both my daughter and granddaughter," William said.

"Only good things, I hope, Dr. O'Malley," James said.

"Of course. Call me William, please. Only my patients call me Doctor."

"What do you specialize in?"

"Psychiatry."

"Would you like to come in and sit down?" Katherine asked.

"No, thank you. We have reservations," James said, perspiration beginning to bead on his forehead. "I don't want to be late."

Chrissie ran into the room. "Mama, I want to go, too."

"Not this time, dear. We have some business to take care of, but I'll be home early," Evelyn said.

"I'll wait up for you so you can tell me a bedtime story," Chrissie said.

Evelyn knelt down in front of Chrissie and hugged her. "Be good for Pa Pa and Grandmommy."

"I'm always good," Chrissie said, grinning.

Evelyn rolled her eyes and glanced at her mother.

"Don't worry about Chrissie," Katherine said. "She's always good for me."

"I'll have Evelyn home early," James said to Mr. and Mrs. O'Malley.

"Enjoy yourself," William said.

They watched as the car drove away.

"Mr. McMann is handsome. He certainly has old-fashioned courtesy. But, I don't feel good about him. There's something wrong," said Katherine.

"He gave her a good deal," William said.

"Too good. Something's up."

William was quiet for a moment. "Did you notice he began to perspire when he found out I was a psychiatrist?"

"I missed that. I hope Evelyn keeps her distance."

"So do I," he said with a sigh.

CHAPTER 3

James watched from the villa across the street. When he saw the tall, handsome, athletically built man with the dark tan, an intense feeling of jealousy raged through him. It was the same man Evelyn had spoken to in the restaurant.

He called Ed and asked him to make an appearance and find out who he was. James paced back and forth across the window, watching. Ed entered the scene, introduced himself, and began carrying in boxes. Damn! That wasn't what he'd asked him to do. Now no one was watching the model. But no one was driving by to look either.

James went into the kitchen, grabbed a Coke from the fridge, added some ice, rum, and a slice of lime. Taking it back into the living room, he glanced out the window again. Both Mr. and Mrs. O'Malley, along with Chrissie, had pulled up to the villa and were carrying clothes and toys in. They stopped, spoke, and laughed with the tall man. A silver Corvette drove up and stopped in front of the villa. *Who's that?* He watched, stunned as Chrissie ran up and threw her arms around the tall, good-looking, dark-haired man that had just gotten out of the Corvette.

When he saw his face, he swore. The one person he never wanted to see in front of Evelyn's villa was here. Thomas Valentino.

The cell phone rang. "Hey, the tall guy's Dan Valentino, Thomas Valentino's brother. Evidently, they're all on good terms, buddy. Thanks for sending me over. Your friend Evelyn's quite a looker. Oh yeah! Thomas Valentino just drove up. Man, if my wife and her friends only knew, we would have a real crowd here."

"Thanks, Ed." If he could have growled, he would have. Instead, he nursed his drink, had another one, and decided if he had half a chance after Thomas left, he'd take Evelyn on a date she'd never forget. After everyone left tonight, he'd pay her a visit, maybe take a pizza and Cokes over for Chrissie and her. But her parents' car, Dan's, and Thomas Valentino's remained parked there until well after midnight.

Pissed off, James turned on the TV, poured another rum and Coke, and drank until he fell asleep. His sleep was disturbed. When he awoke the next morning, he felt as though he hadn't slept at all. Rumpled, still in his clothing, he went out to pick up the morning paper. The headlines startled him:

Second Exotic Dancer Strangled in a Month!
Serial Killer on the Loose?

"Way to go, James!" Steve said.

"What do you mean?"

"You did it, buddy. Don't worry about it. She was asking for it."

"I couldn't have done it. I fell asleep watching TV last night."

"Both of them were working as exotic dancers at night.

Don't you remember? You did it just like you always do it."

"I didn't." He suspected he was lying when a familiar, unsettling feeling overwhelmed him. Fragments of his dream returned. He remembered a surge of sexual excitement and a pair of terror-stricken blue eyes staring into his. He couldn't see the shape of her mouth. She was gagged. Large hands encased in surgical gloves were wrapped around her neck, squeezing the life from her. It was a nightmare, a familiar one.

"Look in your pockets, buddy."

James shoved his hands into his pockets. He frowned and pulled out a pair off red thong underwear.

"What the hell? I don't remember anything. He walked over to the garbage can and tossed the thong in. Maybe he had done it, but if he had, he hadn't been morally responsible for the crime.

He'd blacked out. Whoever had done it had probably done the world a favor. He tied up the trash and took it to the dumpster.

****

"Mommy, we have flowers!" Chrissie said, running into the room. "Hurry, come with me. The man with the flowers is waiting at the door."

Evelyn moved to the bed and set down the stack of plastic hangers she'd taken from her parents' closet. Moving into the living room and into the entry where Chrissie stood, her eyes widened as she saw the lovely bouquet of yellow roses the delivery man at the door held.

"Ms. Valentino?"

"Yes," she said, taking the flowers. "Are these for me?"

"If you're Ms. Valentino, they are."

"I am, and thank you so much," she said.

"Are those from Daddy?" Chrissie asked.

"I don't know, dear," she said, setting the vase down on the dining room table. Peering into the center of the bouquet, she saw a card. Withdrawing it, she read, *To Evelyn and Chrissie, Wishing you a warm welcome to your new home. Enjoy, James.*

"How nice. They are to both of us from James."

Chrissie made a face and said, "From Mr. Stranger Danger, you mean."

"He's been very nice to us, Chrissie," Evelyn said.

"I guess."

That evening, Evelyn called James to thank him. Once again, there was no answer. She left her message on his voicemail along with an invitation to join her Saturday for a tour of Taliesin West.

****

James rose the next morning with a splitting headache again. The bottle of rum was empty. Empty cans of Coke, a vodka bottle, and an empty carton of orange juice rested upside down in the trash. His stomach was churning and he was in no mood for coffee. He showered, dressed, and left for the liquor store.

On his way, he turned on his cell phone. There was a message from Evelyn. He smiled, changed his plans, and headed toward the grocery store for aspirin, healthy food, and a case of beer. As an afterthought, he picked up a bottle of cranberry juice. He had two days to clean out his system and sober up before he saw her. With the binge he'd been on, he needed to detox and do it quick. He hoped he could ward off the D.T.s. Steve had told him if you didn't come off a binge slowly, you could die.

A couple of days later, still feeling a little high, James was sober enough to keep his date with Evelyn. He showered, splashed on his favorite aftershave, and dressed in chinos, loafers without socks, and a pale blue shirt tucked into his trousers. Rolling up the sleeves of his shirt to his elbows, he checked his image in the full-length mirror on the closet. His eyes were clear and he was neat and well dressed for the outing. His headache was gone, but the voices were chattering in his head. He turned and walked out of the villa, determined to keep them muffled. He hadn't taken his meds yet.

****

"Hey, Sunshine. You're looking gorgeous today," he said, observing her. "You should wear that shade of green more often. It really brings out the green in your eyes."

"Thanks," Evelyn said, smiling.

"You're welcome. I've been looking forward to our outing today. I've heard a lot about it."

Once they arrived and began their tour, Evelyn could tell he loved every minute of it. When he'd first arrived to pick her up, she sensed he didn't feel well. There was definitely something wrong, but he hadn't mentioned Taliesin West.

When they finished the tour, he was extraordinarily quiet while walking to the car. "Did you enjoy Taliesin West, James?"

"I enjoyed it immensely. I was just thinking about how much I had wanted to become an architect."

"Why didn't you?" Evelyn asked.

"The usual. Life got in the way and I settled for a business degree. It was what my father wanted. He was killed when I was eighteen just before I began college."

"What happened?"

"He was killed in an accident," he said, not wanting to go into the details. "My mother was dead and I had no one to advise me but my pals Vince and Sal. The three of us have been enormously successful, though. More than likely, I wouldn't have achieved the same degree of financial success as an architect."

She wanted to ask what sort of accident his father had died in, but she sensed this was not the time to discuss it. Instead, she said, "Well, they say never look back. It seems to me you are using your talents anyway."

"How so?" James asked, glancing toward her.

"Simply by the suggestions and changes you've made with the models."

He nodded. "I suppose you're right."

"What did you like best about Taliesin?"

"Everything. I felt like a kid visiting the chocolate factory," he said, grinning.

She laughed. "Good, that's what I was hoping for. I enjoyed it, too."

"If you're free next Friday until around midnight, I'd like to take you someplace special," James said, opening the passenger door to the SUV for her.

"Sounds interesting and mysterious," Evelyn said, turning to face him before she stepped up into the Lexus.

"Do you like to dance?" James asked, gazing into her sparkling hazel eyes.

"Do I like to dance? My absolute favorite thing to do," Evelyn said with a note of pleasure in her voice.

He raised an eyebrow. "Is that so?" he asked, moving closer to her.

The sensual scent of his spicy aftershave lotion drifted toward her, arousing her senses. "Ah, well, almost." She wasn't sure, but she thought his voice and words had a suggestive tone to them. Just thinking of being entwined with James warmed her just as his nearness did. She knew she was blushing and cast her eyes down.

He chuckled and paused a moment. "Will you be able to find someone to watch Chrissie?"

"I think so. Dan has been saying he would like to have her for a weekend. He keeps a little place in Rocky Point, Mexico on the beach. She loves to go down there with him."

"Dan?" James asked.

"My brother-in-law, Chrissie's uncle, Thomas's brother."

"Sounds perfect." His mouth tightened and his jaw clenched. He didn't like the closeness that still existed with the Valentinos. If all went well, what he had planned would draw her closer to him and further away from the Valentinos. "Wear something casual, like capris or jeans; bring along a swimsuit and a sundress, maybe. There will be a place to change."

"Hmmm. Would you like to give me a little hint about where we're going?" Evelyn asked, placing her hand on his forearm.

He shook his head and smiled, his eyes meeting hers. "It's a surprise. I think you'll like it," he said, bending to plant a kiss on the top of her head.

As she leaned into him, he drew her closer. Tilting her chin up, he bent his tall frame. His lips met hers for a long moment. Warmly returning his kiss, sparks seemed to flash between them. Reluctantly breaking their contact, James offered her his hand and said, "Let me help you into the car."

"Thank you, James. You're such a gentleman. I love that."

"You're welcome. But, with a woman like you, how could a man be otherwise?"

Glancing up at him, she smiled appreciatively. Though she knew he was a charmer, she found his words flattering.

"Do you have time to stop for a latte on the way home?" James asked.

"I'd love to, but unfortunately, I really don't have the time."

"Then, I'll look forward to Friday," James said.

****

By the time James picked Evelyn up Friday night, she was well settled into the villa and it appeared she'd been spending nearly every morning in the pool with Chrissie. She was tanned to a near bronzed color. The highlights in her hair had turned a light golden blonde. She looked luscious in the low-cut turquoise top she wore, along with a casual floral skirt that enhanced her gorgeous figure. It was all he could do to keep from running his hand over her firm derriere. Her sandals were attractive but sensible, fine for what he had planned.

"You're looking gorgeous tonight as usual. Do you have a swimsuit with you?"

"Yes. My swimsuit and sundress are in my tote bag. I can't wait to find out where we're going."

"I think you'll like it, at least, I hope so," James said, smiling.

Within a short time, they pulled up to the airport in Scottsdale. A pilot greeted them and led them through security and to the Lear Jet that was owned by JVS Developers.

"Is this your company plane?" she asked, boarding.

Yes," James said. "You're not afraid of flying, are you?"

"No. Not if the pilot is competent."

"We wouldn't have hired him if he weren't," James said. "Take one of the seats in the back of the plane. We'll have more privacy that way," he said, placing his hand on the middle of her back.

"Nice plane," Evelyn said. She was accustomed to flying on private planes. Most that she had flown on with Thomas had been flashier.

He grinned. "We had the interior custom designed."

She sank into the white leather sofa in the rear of the plane and sighed with pleasure.

He took a seat next to her and asked, "A glass of Champagne before we take off?"

"I'd really prefer orange juice. Where are we going?"

"A secret, Sunshine," he said with a wide grin as his azure eyes met hers.

I'm not sure I like secrets. Someone should know where I am going.

****

Once they were in the air and well on their way to their destination, they were offered a selection of hors d'oeuvres and drinks. Evelyn chose orange juice. When she turned away, James added a healthy amount of vodka to it. Thinking he'd better stay on the wagon, he chose an ice-cold Coke minus the rum. Guacamole dip, chips, and salsa were served along with the drinks while Spanish music played softly. Halfway to their destination, Evelyn dozed off, her head resting on James's shoulder.

When she awoke, she gazed into his eyes. Lowering his head, his lips met hers while his fingers traced a path down her long, slim neck toward her breasts. Aroused, he felt her reluctance. He backed off as the pilot requested they fasten their seat belts due to unexpected turbulence ahead.

When they departed the plane, they were rushed through immigration where their citizenship was checked, then into a private car and taken to a remote resort. Set at the base of a mountain range, fifteen to twenty thatched palapas on stilts overlooked a river and estuary. Beyond that was the Pacific Ocean. Near each of the palapas was a rowboat or a canoe.

"Let's go to the lobby first and then the cabana," James said.

"Let's. I'd like to freshen up. My lord. I never expected this, James. I thought you were taking me dancing someplace in Scottsdale. Where in the world are we? It looks like Mexico, somewhere near Puerto Vallarta."

"Close. We're just a little south of Puerto Vallarta in a special hideaway. Not many people know about this spot. The beach is wonderful, the river's gorgeous, the pool and waterfalls are spectacular." "Do you come here often?"

"Occasionally, when I need to escape from civilization."

"Do you ever go to Puerto Vallarta?"

"No, not often. When I come here, it's usually because I want a break from the cities. There's a little town south of here, I like. Jalapa, but I haven't been there for a while. Have you been there?" James asked.

"Yes, but I imagine it's changed a lot. They probably have electricity in the palapas now as well as many visitors."

"I wonder if you can drive there now?" James asked.

"I'm not sure. A bridge may have been built by now. If not, I expect they still have to take a boat or a ferry."

"I'd like to see it…maybe tomorrow. I thought we might take a swim, then maybe have something to eat. Does that sound like something you would like to do?"

James asked.

"Yes, delightful."

"Why don't you take a look at the pool while I take care of registration?" James asked.

"Registration?"

"Yes. We'll need a cabana to change in," James said with a grin.

She drew her brows together. Had he planned to stay overnight? She hadn't arranged for anyone to keep Chrissie that long and she certainly hadn't intended to spend the night. Feeling somewhat uncomfortable, she moved from the lobby through the rustic surroundings of the resort.

The décor was elegant with Mexican-style furnishings. A huge candelabra hung from the center of the beamed ceiling in the dining room while white votive candles rested in the center of each of the round Mexican tables.

Moving out onto the pool area, she gasped in awe of the scenery. On one side of the deck was the Pacific Ocean; on the other, a tropical mountain range thickly covered with palm trees, wild vines, and brush.

"Well, what do you think, gorgeous?" James asked, moving up alongside her.

"It's fantastic. I don't think I have ever seen such an enchanting and unusual resort," Evelyn said. *It's obviously a lover's retreat.*

"Let's have a look at the grounds and then we'll change," James said.

They walked hand-in-hand through the gardens to a mini-zoo containing multi-colored parrots, tropical birds, a jaguar, and a pond with goldfish.

"Have you ever been to a resort with a zoo before, Sunshine?" James asked.

Actually, she had. On one of the first trips she and Thomas had taken, they'd flown a private jet to South America to explore the Rio Negro Tributary, the largest left tributary of the Amazon, it is one of the largest fresh water eco regions in the world. In its deepest waters it is jet black.

After exploring the waters and villages along its banks, they had been guests of the owner of a five-star resort that had an impressive zoo. They'd fallen in love there in Manaus, Brazil. It had been a special time in her life, a private one, one she didn't want to share.

"This is spectacular, James. I especially love the parrots and the jaguar. I'm so glad you brought me here," Evelyn said, avoiding his question.

"Good. I wanted to bring you someplace special," James said.

"You have. Thank you," Evelyn said with appreciation.

Had she not been reminded of Thomas, she might have fallen into the enchanting web he was weaving. She realized when she saw the palapa with its gauze-netted bed, private terrace, and open-air shower he'd meant not only to romance her, but possibly a bit more. Though she'd been too long without love, she still needed to know more about James before she could accept his romantic overtures. Still, it was past time she found someone else. James had brought her to this delightfully romantic place. He was charming, handsome, and had been more than generous to Chrissie and to her.

"The palapas are quiet, a real getaway from civilization, especially if no one knows where you are."

And no one does. What if something happened? There was no way to reach her.

"Do you like it?"

"I've never seen anything like this, but I wish you would have told me where we were going." Not quite trusting James, she said, "I think I'd like to take a swim now."

While Evelyn changed, James stepped to the window and gazed down upon the view. It couldn't have been a more perfect day, except for the heat and humidity. The skies were a brilliant blue dotted with a few clouds. There was a slight breeze from the Pacific. He turned when he heard the bathroom door open. His heart skipped a beat. She wore a melon and green bikini with a simple sarong tied just below her waist. "Don't move. Wait there a second," he said, turning to go back outside. Within minutes, he was back again with a hibiscus. Moving to her side, he placed it behind her ear. "Perfect."

Evelyn moved to the mirror over the small Mexican-style dresser. Her eyes lit with pleasure as she turned to thank him.

"Go on up to the pool now. I'll meet you there after I've changed."

Evelyn walked back to the lodge along the path thinking how spontaneous James had been. Why did she felt uneasy with him? She was attracted to him, no doubt about it. He was considerate and fun to be with except for the few times that he drank too much.

No one was in the lobby as she passed through, nor was anyone at the pool. *It must be off season.* She removed the hibiscus from behind her ear, untied her sarong, and draped it over a chair near an umbrella table. She moved to the side of the large kidney-shaped pool, dove in, and swam straight for the waterfall that tumbled over black lava rocks. Ducking under the falls, she stood on a ledge and ran her fingers through her hair, brushing it back from her face.

****

James walked through the lobby and paused in the entrance to the patio and pool.

Evelyn's sarong was draped over one of the chairs. She was nowhere to be seen. *She should have waited for me.* Even though she could swim well, there was not a lifeguard on duty, nor was anyone around. She could have had a cramp. Not thinking of anything else, he slipped out of his shirt, tossed it onto a chair, dove in, and swam toward the falls. He ducked under, hoping to see Evelyn. When he rose from the water, he saw her standing just beyond the falls, her hair wet and streaming down. He approached her and said, "I was concerned about you. You should have waited."

"I'm sorry. I really didn't think about it," Evelyn said.

"You're gorgeous," James said, moving closer to her. "Cold?"

"A little."

He drew her into his arms and moved his large hands over her back in an effort to warm her. Aroused, he placed his knee between her legs, pushing them apart.

Feeling his strong arousal, Evelyn backed up and said, "I think I'd better get out of the pool and dry off."

He took her hand and pulled her back and into his arms. Bending, his lips met hers. His kiss probed and demanded more. Pushing him away, she scrambled out of the pool, shivering. "I'm not ready for that, James."

"Sorry. You are so beautiful. I just got carried away. You can't blame me for that," he said with a false smile.

"Just this once, I'll forgive you, but slow down."

His smile faded and he clenched his jaw.

"Pissed off, aren't you, buddy? You should have taken her. She's a teaser, just like a lot of the others you've been with. Don't let her get away with it. You're alone here with her except for the meager staff. Hey, you and your partners own the place. You can get away with anything here. You have before."

"I'd like to have something warm to drink, like hot tea," Evelyn said.

"Give her a hot toddy heavily laced with booze, buddy...a couple of them."

"Good idea. There's a restaurant ahead. Let me help you over the steps." Taking her hand in his, he helped her up the steep stone steps. She tripped on the last one. Catching her in his arms, he held her tightly. "Stubbed your toe, too, didn't you?"

She nodded.

"Come on. I'll carry you to the terrace," he said, sweeping her up into his arms. "The stones won't bother me. I'm accustomed to walking on shells. In Florida, I walk on the beach most every morning. It helps me think more clearly. You must visit me in Florida someday soon," James said.

Once the Tiki Hut was in sight, he set her down on the terrace. Bending, he kissed her lightly on her cheek and said, "Let's have a bite and maybe later a nap on the terrace."

A nap? she thought. *With one eye open.*

"Wait right here while I find a couple of beach towels," James said.

"Thanks," she said, wrapping the oversized towel around her shoulders.

"Better?"

She nodded.

"The menu's limited, but the fruit salad's delicious; so are the hamburgers and grouper sandwiches."

"A grouper sandwich sounds good," Evelyn said, her stomach rumbling.

"I think you need a warm meal and a stiff drink to revive you."

"Sounds perfect, but a hot drink, like tea or coffee would be fine."

"I'll order," he said, rising.

She watched him as he moved to the Tiki Hut to order. Tall and tanned, his body was lean, more like a runner's than someone who worked out with weights in a gym. He was handsome and sexy to say the least.

Whatever he had ordered, it hadn't taken long to prepare it. He set the hot drinks topped with whipped cream on the table. "It's steaming hot. Just sip it."

"Mmm. This drink is delicious. What is it?"

"I thought you would like it. It's one of their specialties," he said. The corners of his mouth turned up.

"It tastes different. Does it have alcohol in it?"

"Maybe a little."

"I thought so."

The waitress set their lunches on the table. Evelyn was famished. She forgot about the fact that she hadn't wanted an alcoholic drink. She forced herself to eat slowly and not devour the sandwich and potato salad that was served with it.

"Good?"

"Mmm. The best."

"What do you like to do in your spare time besides dance?"

"Ride horses, play tennis, swim, and I love boating when I'm near a lake or the sea."

"I enjoy boating too. When you come to Florida, we'll take the yacht out. What do you read?"

"Romantic suspense mostly, and adventure novels."

"I like adventure novels. So does my son, Bobby. He's written some articles about some of our fishing trips."

"That's impressive."

"He's good. You would like him."

"I'm sure I would."

After lunch, they walked back to their palapa. Though she hadn't planned to, she fell asleep almost immediately in a hammock that hung on the deck overlooking the Pacific. She awoke several hours later to find James had fallen asleep in the gauze-netted bed inside the bungalow. Michael Crichton's latest book lay beside him. Two empty bottles of Corona sat on the floor near the end table. Quietly, she took a beach towel from the linen closet and left, making her way down to the beach.

She sat down on the sugar white sand and gazed out to sea, thinking about her life. Even with her parents and Chrissie around her, she was lonely, but not afraid to be alone. Still, she needed the special love and affection only a man she loved could give her. She was drawn to James, and even though she didn't completely trust him, she had become more involved with him than she'd planned to. She still did not know much about him. Up until now, there hadn't been that many men in her life; only Mike, who she'd been briefly engaged to in college, then Thomas.

****

James awoke. Glancing onto the patio, he saw that the hammock Evelyn had fallen asleep in was empty. He rose, moved out onto the patio and gazed out to sea. Evelyn was sitting on the beach. From this distance, she looked like a little girl. He considered joining her, but changed his mind.

He slipped a shirt on and decided Evelyn might enjoy walking down to the beach at sunset to see the baby turtles being released. Afterwards, she could shower and change…a late dinner and dancing maybe. His imagination took off from here only to be interrupted by a cheerful voice.

"Sorry, I'm late. The beach was marvelous, but I stayed a little too long, I think," Evelyn said. "My back is stinging. I'm probably a bit sunburned."

"Turn around and I'll check."

She turned around, her back to him.

"You're a little red, but I don't think you will burn. If it still hurts after you shower off, I'll put some aloe on your back. I have some with me."

"I doubt I'll need it."

"I was tempted to join you, but decided you might want some time to yourself."

"I'd have enjoyed your company, but thank you for your consideration. Would you mind if I shower now?" Evelyn asked.

"Not at all. I'll stay out here. My book will entertain me, but not nearly as well as you do."

She laughed and said, "I won't be long."

"You won't be able to dry your hair," James said.

"Then air drying will just have to do. As long as there's soap and a towel, that will be all I need."

He heard the shower and was struck with a flash of pure arousal. He rose and moved into the cabana, stopping just short of the bathroom door.

"Go for it. Now's your chance."

Steve's right. But, I'll never achieve my long-term goal that way. Not with her. With more self-control than he thought possible, he turned around, reclined on the bed, and opened his book. The shower stopped. He saw her clothes laid out on the chair.

"Oh! I thought you were outside," Evelyn said, moving into the front room.

"Sorry. I had a slight headache and came in to lie down. Don't worry, I'll close my eyes."

His heart pounded as he watched, his eyes half-closed. She wore nothing but a small towel wrapped around her. His fantasies went wild. He visualized her moving toward him, bending down to kiss his forehead while the towel slipped to the floor. He was off his meds and still sober. He wanted her more now than he had at the pool. He wanted to take her hand and draw her down onto the bed. But, he knew she wasn't ready for that.

A strong knock came at the door, jolting him out of his daydream.

"Who is it?" James asked.

"Sal."

"Wait a second," James said.

"I'll get dressed," Evelyn said, moving to the chair to retrieve her clothing and carrying them into the small bath. She had planned to dress in the other room since the bathroom was so small and there was no place to hang her dress. *This is going to be awkward.* With one hand, she held onto the dress. With the other, she unfastened her towel and let it drop to the floor. The hem of her sundress fell into water that had dripped onto the floor.

Irritated that James had moved into the front room from the patio, she quickly slipped into the garment. After she had scrunched her wavy hair, she applied lipstick, gloss, blush, and mascara. Moving into the front room, she slipped her shoes on. She wondered if he'd lied about the headache. His arousal had been apparent. He couldn't have hidden it if he'd wanted to. Had he intended to join her in the shower, then changed his mind at the last minute?

"I'm sorry. I didn't know Sal and his girlfriend were coming down. They will meet you in the lounge while I shower and dress," James said.

"I'm looking forward to meeting them. How will they know me?"

"I told him to look for the prettiest blonde in the restaurant; petite, nice figure, nice tan, sexy black sundress, and heels," James said.

She smiled, shook her head, and left for the restaurant.

****

Sal and his woman of the moment took their time exploring the mini-zoo and the grounds. When they entered the lounge, his heart skipped a beat. Evelyn was sitting at table alone in the softly lit lounge. She looked familiar. He smiled and remembered where he'd met her. She was looking better than ever. James was a lucky guy. Sensual Spanish music played in the background, adding to the ambiance.

"Will you excuse me, Sal? I'd like to go into the ladies room for a minute."

"Take your time, babe," Sal said as he moved into the lounge to Evelyn's table. "Evelyn Valentino, I'm Sal Catalano, James's partner. May I join you?"

Surprised, she glanced up from the menu she'd been perusing. The handsome stranger who had just introduced himself was darkly tanned, of medium height, and well built. "It's so nice to meet you, Mr. Catalano. Please, do sit down and join me. I'm waiting for James. How did you know my name?" Evelyn asked.

"I stopped by the palapa. James described you, but I

would have known you anywhere."

"Oh? Have I met you somewhere before? You look familiar."

"I lived in Las Vegas several years ago. While I was working on a project there with my uncle, I met Thomas Valentino. We became casual friends and I met you once at one of his shows. I have never forgotten either of you. I was sorry to hear of your divorce."

"Thank you for saying that. It was so public," Evelyn said. Humiliation was apparent in the tone of her voice.

"It was. That must have been embarrassing to you both," Sal said.

She nodded.

"I always liked Thomas. I was surprised to read about the scandal. He didn't seem to be that kind of man," Sal said.

"I know. It was a surprise to me."

"And now you're seeing James. You haven't known him long, have you?"

"A few months. He's been very kind to me and to my daughter."

"James has a big heart. I don't know you and probably shouldn't mention it, but he is quite smitten with you. Do you feel the same about him?"

"Why are you asking?"

"Because I've known James a long time, since he was eleven years old. I just wondered how much he had told you about himself," Sal said.

Evelyn drew her brows together. *Is there something he's trying to tell me?* "Actually, he's told me a lot but nothing, if you know what I mean. Apparently, his wife and parents were all killed in accidents. He told me his wife was killed in an auto accident. I don't know how his mother or his father was killed. He's young to be so alone."

"So you really don't know much about him yet," Sal said.

"He remains a mystery to me," Evelyn said. "I'd like to know more about him. I'm attracted to James and I do like him."

"Ask away. It will be between us."

"My parents are concerned that perhaps James may be more than just a social drinker, for one," Evelyn said.

"That's a valid concern. Keep him away from the booze. If you and James become serious, there's something else you should know, something he probably won't tell you."

I knew it. "And that is?" Evelyn asked.

"Later. He's here," Sal said.

****

James stood at the entrance to the lounge, his hands knotted into tight balls. Sal was sitting with Evelyn, chatting with her as though he'd known her forever. His girlfriend, whatever her name was, wasn't with him. He moved to the table. "Talking about me?"

"You surprised me. I thought you would be longer," Evelyn said, ignoring his question.

"Evidently. Where's your girlfriend, Sal?" James asked.

"She's in the ladies room. Oh, here she comes," Sal said.

During dinner, Evelyn thought about her brief conversation with Sal. She wished they had had more time to finish their talk. She felt as though there was something important he had wanted to tell her about James, something he couldn't say in front of him. It couldn't have been good. She was glad she had not become physically involved with him yet.

On their way back from the resort, James felt Evelyn drawing away from him. He wondered what Sal had said. There was any number of things he didn't want Evelyn to know. He'd been immediately attracted to her. She'd proven to be an excellent companion. An intriguing conversationalist, she was not a chatterbox. He had fallen in love with her almost immediately, but sensed he could not rush her. She'd been hurt badly by her former husband and unfortunately, he thought she might still be in love with him. What he needed was a miracle.

****

During what seemed to be a long, hot week to James, he stopped by the grocery store to pick up a *Wall Street Journal*, the daily paper, and a few groceries. While he stood waiting at the checkout counter, his eyes were drawn to the headlines of a popular tabloid. *Superstars in Love*. Pictured on the front page was Thomas Valentino in a warm embrace with the actress and dance star, Julie Moss. James grinned. A miracle had happened. He couldn't resist. He picked up a copy of the tabloid and paid for his purchases.

On Wednesday night, he called Evelyn and invited her and Chrissie to go to Disneyland. They would take the Lear and would be home by Chrissie's bedtime Saturday night. Evelyn was delighted and knew Chrissie would be, too. They were to meet at the villa James was staying in at 8:30 a.m.

When Evelyn and Chrissie arrived, they were invited in. James wasn't quite ready to leave. Pouring them both orange juice and offering them a scone, he left the room.

"Mommy! Look! It's Daddy and Julie!"

"What?" Evelyn asked, leaning over to see the paper Chrissie held. Stunned, Evelyn felt flushed, dizzy. She hadn't known Thomas was involved with anyone. As recently as last week, he'd called and asked her to fly over and visit. He'd said that he wanted to get back together again, that he'd never been unfaithful to her. It had all been a terrible mistake. Her blood ran cold.

"Mommy, do you see Daddy?" Chrissie asked, handing her the paper.

"Yes. Do you know Julie Moss, Chrissie?"

"She's my friend, Mommy. I like her. She's pretty and I want to sing and dance just like she does when I grow up. You're pretty too, Mommy, but Julie's skin is darker and she doesn't need to sit by the beach or the pool to be tan. She's not Italian like Daddy either."

"I believe everyone in the world has heard of Julie Moss, dear. If I'm right, she's from Louisiana, a beautiful Creole woman, as well as a wonderful entertainer and singer. I just didn't know she was a friend of Daddy's or that you knew her."

"She's nice, Mommy. You would like her. Maybe you will meet her sometime. What is Creole?"

"A Creole is a descendant of the French or Spanish and of the African-American. You are a descendant of the Irish and Italian."

"I love to hear Julie talk," Chrissie said. "Her voice is so soft and she says her words differently."

"Creoles have spoken a mixture of French and Spanish for generations," Evelyn said. "And they do have a beautiful accent."

"Her skin is so dark and pretty. It's softer than yours or Daddy's. Is that because she is Creole?" Chrissie asked.

"Probably so," Evelyn said. She was so thankful that

Chrissie didn't have a prejudice bone in her little body. Neither she nor Thomas did either, but her great-grandmother, who had been raised in the South, had been quite prejudice.

Evelyn sighed. She had no holds on Thomas. There was no reason he shouldn't be seeing someone. She was. She should have given Thomas a chance to explain their misunderstanding, as he called it. He'd denied that he'd ever been unfaithful to her. Now, it was too late. Obviously, he was interested in someone else now. She was glad that he was with someone Chrissie liked. They'd been divorced two years.

"Evelyn, Chrissie, are you ready?" James, asked, wearing a wide grin on his handsome face.

"I'm ready," Chrissie said, going for the door. "Come on, Mommy."

Evelyn set the paper down and followed.

****

They had a wonderful time at Disneyland. It was all James could do but hum "Everything's Going My Way." He'd made up his mind. Evelyn was going to be his wife, if she'd have him. She would, he promised himself. The only things he'd need to do would be to win Chrissie's affections, curb his drinking habits, hide a bit of his past, and keep the voices at bay…voices that told him Evelyn was no better than Elaine.

CHAPTER 4

James crunched the beer can and tossed it on top of several dozen others in the kitchen waste basket. He still hadn't had his prescription filled or taken his meds. He'd blacked out again. Now he had a killer of a hangover. He wasn't sure what had happened or where he'd been except that a matchbook from a local strip joint was lying on his coffee table. His shirt collar had bright red lipstick on it and he'd found a black, lacy thong, size 5, in his pants pocket. The evidence spoke all, at least he hoped so. He'd thrown the thong in the trash.

James picked up the paper and began to read it. Perspiration beaded on his forehead. Local stripper strangled. He read on. Just like the last time, she'd been a college girl, working to pay her way through school. Running his hands through his hair, he wondered where the girl had worked. He picked up the matchbook and read the cover. Then he read the article again. Same place. The Oasis Gentleman's Club. Her name was Elaine.

"You did it, man. Just like you did it here a couple of weeks ago and in Pompano Beach and Ft. Lauderdale last year. Gotta hand it to you, buddy. You never leave any clues and they all deserved what they got," Steve said.

"Shit, Steve. This girl was working her way through school. She didn't deserve anything."

"Sure, she did. She was selling herself, wasn't she? Just like the rest."

"No. I wouldn't do that, not in my right mind." He shook his head. He had to pull himself together before he hurt someone he loved. He'd never win Evelyn this way. Maybe it was a coincidence. Maybe he hadn't killed her. Someone else had. Steve, maybe. Not him. He picked up the paper again and stared at her picture. She looked familiar. Maybe she'd given him a lap dance. That would explain the lipstick on his shirt. But the thong? Maybe he'd taken a girl home.

But, what about Pompano? He vaguely remembered that. At the time, there had been stranglings up and down the beach on A1A between Ft. Lauderdale and Delray. They'd never caught the guy. He'd had a lot of blackouts, found thongs of various sizes and colors in the pockets of his trousers. Where had he put them? He remembered. He'd thrown them all into the trash. He was a drunk, but not a killer. He was sure of that.

He needed and wanted Evelyn. Physically, he wouldn't be able to make love to her in this condition, whether he wanted to or not. Next week, he'd return to Florida for at least a week or two. Bobby had some time off and he wanted Evelyn to meet him. The boy needed a mother, one that would love him and that he would accept. He hadn't been much of a father.

Maybe he did have a chemical imbalance as the doctors had said he did. He couldn't tell when the voices were real or not. The doctors said they weren't, that the hallucinations weren't real either. Since he'd been in his late teens, he'd heard voices and seen hideous things like trolls in his closet. Sometimes, they lurked in dark corners and waited for him. No one else saw them. When he took his meds, it was better. The voices quieted down and the hallucinations stopped.

But, he didn't feel like himself. He gained weight and lost his sexual desire. He chose not to take the medicine. When the symptoms occurred again, he drank until he blacked out. He'd been arrested many times for violent things he'd done or tried to do. Sal and Vince had always bailed him out. He was afraid he might not live long or that he'd do something bad when he was off his meds.

He looked for his prescription, but couldn't find it. Raising the phone, he punched in the doctor's number. He needed to stabilize, at least for the time he was in close proximity to Evelyn and until she married him. He'd have her then. There would be no turning back for her.

CHAPTER 5

Evelyn needed a break. The shock of seeing the headlines in the tabloid and Thomas's picture with Julie Moss had been more than Evelyn could tolerate. For the past week, she'd been unfocused, irritable, and unable to sleep. James hadn't called since they had returned from Disneyland. She rose from the laptop after sitting in front of it for a half hour without writing a word. She needed to snap out of it. She was developing writer's block.

By evening, she had dropped Chrissie off at her parents' home and was dining with her sister Lainey at her home in Sedona, a beautiful and spiritual place. After telling her all about James, Lainey suggested she have a reading and take a vision quest.

"That's something I've always wanted to do," Evelyn said.

"You've had readings before, haven't you?"

"Astrological, but not a reading by a mystic."

"Running Deer is both an astrologer and a medium. He won't be giving you a psychic reading per se. The astrology reading he does will be to check the timing of the vision quest, whether it will be beneficial, and whether or not you may encounter danger in the wilderness at this time," Lainey said. "Running Deer is in tune with the spirits. Those who wish to give you a message will do so through him."

"When can we do this?" Evelyn asked.

"He's coming to dinner tomorrow night. We'll ask him then."

"Hmm. Is he your new love interest?" Evelyn asked with a mischievous grin.

"How did you guess?"

"I knew there was someone new. You haven't been down to Phoenix for a while. We've missed you."

"It doesn't sound to me like you've had much time to miss me," Lainey said with a grin.

"James has kept me busy."

"Too busy for your writing and meditation?" Lainey asked, raising a brow.

"I'm afraid so," Evelyn said, not wanting to admit her failure. They had both been taught at an early age to set aside time to meditate daily.

"Tomorrow morning, we're going for a hike, and when we come back, we're going to meditate. Then writing, if you feel like it can come later, before dinner," Lainey said.

"I can't think of anything more pleasant." Evelyn said, smiling warmly.

If Lainey hadn't told her of her feelings for Running Deer, Evelyn would have known from the moment he entered Lainey's home that he was far more than an interesting new man to her. The chemistry between the two almost bounced off the walls. He was of medium height, slender, with thick, coal-black, shoulder-length hair. His eyes were dark blue, his nose straight and narrow while his complexion was smooth and medium in shade. He was of Native American descent to be sure. But of which tribe, she didn't know, nor could she begin to guess his other genes. He was one of the most handsome men she'd ever seen.

"I've heard a lot about you, Evelyn. It's a pleasure to meet you," Running Deer said.

"And you, Running Deer."

"Lainey tells me you are interested in taking a vision quest."

"Yes. I believe I may have some difficult decisions coming up soon. I thought a vision quest would be beneficial at this time."

"How much do you know about them?" Running Deer asked.

"When I went to the boarding school here in Sedona, many of my friends told me about the vision quests they had taken."

"So you know that you must fast and camp out alone in a medicine wheel made of stones that you have created for two to four days. You need to know first aid."

Evelyn nodded.

"Do you play a musical instrument like a drum or a flute that you would like to bring with you?"

"I have an Indian Drum and a flute."

"Then bring them," Running Deer said.

"How do you feel about being in the wilderness alone?" Lainey asked. "I know that as a child, you were afraid of wild animals."

"I still am," Evelyn said.

"Neither Lainey nor I can be with you. You need to be alone during this journey of the spirit. Are you all right with that?"

"Will someone be nearby?"

"Running Deer was camped nearby when I took my vision quest," Lainey said.

"Then you weren't all alone."

"It seemed like it."

"I will camp out about a mile or two away. You will leave a stone between the two camps every morning," Running Deer said.

"That's not so bad," Evelyn said. "I think I can do that, but what if a cougar or wolves come down to my camp?"

Running Deer chuckled. "That's one of the reasons I want to do an astrological reading for you. I want to make certain that you will be safe."

"Thank God."

Running Deer laughed again. "You know that Astrology is not a means of fortune telling, nor is it fate. We all have free will to do as we please."

Evelyn nodded. "Of course. If something happens and if it's my time to go, nothing will make a difference."

"That's right. Lainey tells me you haven't kept up with your meditation," Running Deer said as though he was scolding her.

She sighed. "No, I haven't. I've spent nearly all of my free time with others recently."

"Mostly one by the name of James, I believe," Lainey said.

Evelyn nodded.

"It would be nice if you had time for a sweat lodge ceremony before you go on the vision quest."

"I don't think I have time," Evelyn said.

"It won't matter. Maybe next time. I'll need your birth date, time of birth, and city you were born in. We'll do the spirit reading tonight, and tomorrow I'll construct your chart. If it's a good time for you, we'll go ahead with the vision quest. If not, we'll plan it for another time. Sound all right?"

She nodded.

After dinner, Running Deer retired alone to Lainey's art studio to meditate for a half hour before he did the spirit reading. When he was ready for Evelyn, he stepped into the living room where she and Lainey had been talking. Following him into the studio, she sat across from him at a round table covered with a white silk cloth. A white candle was lit in the center of the table.

"I need to hold something like a ring that you wear often."

Evelyn glanced at the antique jade ring on her left hand that Thomas had given her. Slipping it off her finger, she placed it in his hand.

He took a deep breath and said, "Someone who means a lot to you gave this to you."

She nodded.

"This person will always be in your life," Running Deer said.

If only for Chrissie, I hope so.

Running Deer closed his eyes. Minutes later, he said, "All is not as it may seem. There are many things happening behind the scenes that you are not aware of. Someone, a man, is misrepresenting himself."

Thomas. He betrayed me.

"You may think it is someone that it is not. You are being deceived even now." Running Deer was quiet for a few minutes. His brows came together and he grimaced. "Something reeks. It smells rotten. If you are not careful, you may find yourself facing a life or death situation."

Evelyn shivered. "How can I avoid this?"

He opened his eyes and said, "By hearing the truth.

Meditate and pray that you will be able to make wise decisions. The time is nearly at hand."

"Thank you, I will be careful."

After spending a week with Lainey, Evelyn left, disappointed that she had not been able to take the vision quest. Running Deer had said Neptune in transit was afflicting her natal Mercury and that her judgment was clouded and would be for some months to come. Another factor that played in strongly against the vision quest was that Mercury was going into its retrograde position for three weeks. That, in itself, was enough for Running Deer to warn her against a vision quest. Though often described as a courageous journey, her quest for truth and purpose must be taken at another time.

CHAPTER 6

Evelyn had just arrived home. Once she had unpacked, she decided to go for a swim before she picked Chrissie up. Taking a turquoise bikini from the bottom drawer of her dresser, she put it on and tied a matching sarong around her waist. She slid into her sandals and took Stuart Wood's latest novel from her bedside table to read.

After swimming a dozen laps, Evelyn stepped out of the pool and stretched out in a comfortable recliner under a large palm tree. Her bathing suit dried quickly in the searing heat. She took a can of ice cold lemonade out of the cooler and set it on the table beside her. Thirsty, she opened it, took a gulp, and began to read. No more than five pages later, she heard a familiar voice.

"Hey, gorgeous."

"James. What a nice surprise to see you at the pool."

"You don't come out often," James said.

"I've been out of town and, anyway, I'm usually too busy to come out. Would you like a lemonade?"

"Yes. Thanks. It's hot today."

"Very," she said, taking another can of lemonade from her small cooler.

He opened it, took a long gulp, and said, "I'm going to be leaving for Florida next weekend for a short time. It's hot down there this time of year, too, but I'm hoping you might consider coming along. I'd like you to meet my son, Bobby. Of course, you will have your own suite. You can bring your laptop too, if you like."

"That's very nice of you to invite me, James. I'd love to meet your son and I'd like to go with you. The only thing is, I'll need to ask Dan if he can keep Chrissie while I'm gone," Evelyn said in an uncertain tone.

"I'd like to leave on Saturday and return the following week on Sunday. If that works out, let me know," James said. He knew he'd approached her at a weak moment and had left her alone for more than a week. He was sober now and back on meds. She was down, feeling badly because of her ex-husband's romance with the popular Vegas star, and here he was, ready to sweep her away.

"I'll see what I can do," Evelyn said.

Smiling widely, James walked back to his temporary living quarters. He whistled his lucky song, "Everything's Going My Way."

****

Evelyn packed, happily humming, "On a Clear Day." Everything had worked out perfectly. Much to her surprise, Dan had agreed to keep Chrissie while she went to Florida with James. He had just picked her up and she and James were leaving this afternoon. It would be fun to meet James's son and Vince. She hoped Sal would be there. Maybe then they could continue their conversation about James. In any case, she was looking forward to seeing James's home on the beach. She loved the beach and had always enjoyed trips to visit Lainey at her townhouse in Vero Beach in the winter.

Once more, they were taking the Lear rather than a commercial airline. On the way down, they watched a DVD starring Johnny Depp. It seemed appropriate for their trip to Florida. When they arrived, a limo was waiting for them. Stocked with delicious sandwiches and fine wine, they dined on the way to James's home in Highland Beach.

"Bobby will be waiting for us at the house, Sunshine. He's been looking forward to meeting you," James said with a wide grin on his face.

"Good. I'm looking forward to meeting him, too," Evelyn said.

"How do you feel about deep sea fishing?"

"I love it. I've been a few times with Dad. Oh, I can't say I'm much of a fisherman, but it's fun."

"Have you caught anything?"

"Actually, I did. A marlin, but not as big as the one Dad caught."

"That's great. Bobby loves to go fishing. So do I. I'm thinking of arranging a deep sea fishing trip and taking Bobby, Sal, Vin, his wife, and you, of course."

"Sounds wonderful," she said.

****

She had no idea when he said he was arranging a deep sea fishing trip that they were going to Bimini. There was nothing James didn't do in a big way, including catching marlin. He caught the largest. Except for Sal, everyone on board caught either a marlin or a barracuda. She hooked onto a huge marlin that nearly got away. It would have, maybe with her too, except that Bobby helped her bring it in.

James had arranged a cottage to stay overnight in on the island. Upon arrival, she wondered what the sleeping arrangements would be. So far, James had not pressed her or made advances further than a few rather passionate kisses. She didn't think he would this time either.

She was right. James took a room of his own, Sal another, while Vince and his wife took the master bedroom. As for Bobby, he claimed the sofa in the living room while she happily took the daybed on the screened-in porch facing the ocean.

After everyone had gone to bed, she padded out to the kitchen to make a cup of Chamomile tea. Soon, Bobby joined her at the table.

"Would you like a cup of herb tea, Bobby?"

"What kind?"

"Chamomile. It doesn't have caffeine in it and it will help you sleep."

He nodded. "Is that why you're making it?"

"Partly."

"Sometimes I can't sleep either. That's when I read or write."

"Your dad tells me you write articles."

"Some. But I like to write stories too."

"Fiction?"

"Adventure fiction and non-fiction. I'd like to be a journalist…like Peter Jennings was."

"Impressive. How does your dad feel about your ambitions?"

"I don't think he takes me seriously. He wants me to get a degree in business when I go to college."

"Maybe he will change his mind."

"Maybe. Do you like my dad?"

"Yes."

"Good. I'd like to see you more."

"I would like that, too."

After they had finished their tea, she went back to the screened-in porch, climbed into the daybed, and fell asleep. When she awoke, she took a long walk on the beach. Contemplating her relationship with James, she wondered what would come of it. Though she found herself attracted to him, she wondered what his intentions toward her were. Perhaps he hadn't decided or was just giving her space.

"Evelyn. Wait up," a man yelled.

She stopped, turned, and waved at Sal who was running down the beach toward her.

"So, you're an early riser, too," she said.

"Yeah. But I need coffee when I wake up. I didn't want to putter around in the kitchen making it. There's a bait shop just across the street that has the best coffee I've ever had," Sal said.

"How far is it?"

"Just up ahead. We can cross over at the next path that leads to the road."

James heard the screen door shut for the second time. Rising, he peeked out the verticals. Sal. He'd bet Evelyn had been the first to leave. Pulling on his trunks, he moved into the dressing room and splashed water on his face. After he'd brushed his teeth, he ran a comb through his hair.

"*Hurry, man,*" he heard Steve say. "*Sal's after her.*"

Leaving out the side door, James ran down the beach. "Hey, hold on up there," he hollered.

"I was hoping we would have time to talk," Evelyn said.

"Afraid not," Sal said. "James must have built-in radar."

****

On the way back from Florida, James drew the curtains in their rear cabin, offering them more privacy. He selected soft romantic music and opened a bottle of Champagne. Pouring two glasses, he offered her one.

Taking a sip, he said, "I've been waiting for a moment of privacy all week, Sunshine."

"In spite of the lack of privacy, I loved the trip, especially meeting Bobby and getting to know him."

"I was hoping for that. He means the world to me," James said with deep affection in his voice.

"I could tell. He loves you very much."

"I'm all he has. He adored you," James said, smiling at Evelyn fondly.

"He's a wonderful boy. He looks very much like you."

"Do you think so?"

Evelyn heard the unmistakable note of pleasure in James's voice. "Absolutely. He is so smart and handsome."

"So you think I'm handsome?" James asked, beaming.

"Definitely."

"Mmm," he murmured, taking her into his arms. "You know, Sunshine, that I've fallen in love with you."

Stunned, she didn't know what to say. She'd never love again, not like she had loved Thomas, but he was with someone else now and would never be in her life again.

"Oh, James, you're a wonderful man and I am attracted to you…"

"Shh. You don't need to say anything. I have a little something for you, something I hope you will accept. It belonged to my mother."

Dear God, don't let it be an engagement ring. I don't want to be alone for the rest of my life, but I don't know if I want to marry James either.

James reached into his pocket and pulled out a small box wrapped in glossy pink paper and tied with a narrow gold ribbon. He placed it into her hand, sat back, and watched while she opened the box.

Evelyn's hand trembled as she slowly unwrapped the gift. Her eyes widened as she opened the box.

"Oh, James. This is exquisite. I don't think I've ever seen such a beautiful ring, but I really can't accept it."

"Consider it a gift of our friendship, but while you're wearing it, at least think about spending the rest of your life with me. Let me know when you're ready to move our relationship up a couple of notches."

She nearly groaned aloud. Was this what Running Deer had meant when he had said the time was nearly at hand? She wished she would have found time to speak with Sal so that they could resume their conversation.

CHAPTER 7

Evelyn flashed the four-carat antique diamond ring in front of her mother's eyes while they were waiting for the sopapillas and honey to arrive.

"What do you think, Mom? Isn't it gorgeous?"

Katherine shook her head and gasped. "My God! It's fantastic, but please don't tell me you've accepted a proposal of marriage from that man you met. . .the one who owns the villa you leased. He went a little overboard on the size of the diamond, don't you think, dear? Or is it a cubic zirconium in an antique setting?"

Evelyn laughed. "No, Mother, it's a real diamond. I'm sure of it. James said the ring belonged to his mother. He hasn't proposed; it is a friendship ring. When I decide, if I do, that I would like to move our relationship up a level, then I may consider it an engagement ring."

"It looks like he's trying to coerce you to marry him with his money. Why, it's a far larger stone that your father gave me when we became engaged."

"Your ring is lovely. Wasn't Dad in medical school?"

"Oh yes. I wasn't berating your father. I love my ring, but I've always loved him more. My ring may not be a four-carat diamond in an exquisite antique setting, but your father is a wonderful man."

"The finest, and I think James is, too. The only thing that I'm concerned about is his drinking, but he's slowed down a lot."

"What did you say his last name was? I must not have paid much attention when I met him. More than likely, I probably didn't think you would see him again."

"His last name is McMann, Mother. You've met him several times. Remember when I signed the lease to the condo, he came to pick me up at the house? Later on, James and I had dinner with you and Dad in Scottsdale."

"I vaguely remember him. He never had much to say."

Remembering the occasion, Evelyn couldn't help but smile. They'd just returned from his home in Florida. She'd known when she'd agreed to go that their relationship would move to another level. She'd fallen in love with Bobby, his son, and felt strongly about James who had proven to be a generous and sensitive man. She hoped her parents would accept him.

James had made reservations at one of the finest Chinese restaurants in Scottsdale. She'd worn a sage green silk dress with a relatively short skirt that was slit to the thigh on one side. When she sat down, it had crept up. James had been distracted. He became nervous and, glancing down at her rising skirt, he whispered in her ear, "Pull your skirt down. The man at the next table is staring at you." He'd become irritated and hadn't been at his best as far as conversation was concerned. It wasn't his best point. She'd found his possessiveness amusing.

"Evelyn, are you with me?" Katherine asked.

"I'm sorry, Mother. I was thinking of the last time we had dinner together with James. James McMann. He's here from Boca Raton, Florida, in regard to his business interests in Paradise Valley. Remember?"

Katherine O'Malley shook her head and sighed deeply. "I do now. You haven't known him long, though, not long enough to become engaged to him."

"I've known him for nearly four months, Mother. He's charming, fun, and handsome. I absolutely love being with him."

"But what do you know about him other than the fact that he's a good-looking, tall Irishman with eyes the color of the sea, dimples, and wavy dark hair?"

Evelyn grinned. "I've been to his home in Boca, met his son, his partners, his friends, and taken a tour of his extensive properties, all but the resort in the Bahamas. He's well-off. His hotels are gorgeous, well run, and profitable. So are his apartment complexes, not to mention his sub-divisions."

"I see. But you're mostly telling me about his material possessions."

"You should see his home! Well, you will, when you and Dad visit. It's between Boca Raton and Delray, right off A1A. It's pale yellow with turquoise shutters and a tin roof…Key West style. It sits on a hill or dune and looks over the Atlantic Ocean. The landscaping is gorgeous, lush, with tall, elegant royal palms, bougainvillea, huge sea grapes, nearly as tall as a tree, and oleander plants everywhere. There's a tennis court, of course, and a swimming pool that faces the ocean. It's even nicer than your home in Paradise Valley. Oh! Chrissie will love it."

"You need to think about how she will feel if or when you marry James. As I recall, she called him Mr. Stranger Danger when you met. She is Catholic, like Thomas. You must raise her as one."

Evelyn laughed. "Yes, of course. As far as Chrissie calling James Mr. Stranger Danger, well, Thomas did an excellent job with Chrissie. She refuses to have anything to do with strangers. But James is doing his best to win her over."

Katherine raised an eyebrow. "With dolls and a trip to Disneyland?"

"I think it's kind and considerate of him to consider Chrissie."

"How do you think Thomas will feel if you marry James? You do share split custody of Chrissie. He won't like it when he hears you are marrying a man you've only known four months."

"Thomas! He may be Chrissie's father, but you can't exactly call a womanizer a model husband or father."

"Maybe he wasn't a model husband, but he loves Chrissie dearly. There's not one thing he wouldn't do for her. I don't think you could ask for more. You were too hasty when you divorced him."

"Mother, Thomas's fame and charisma, not to mention his incredible good looks, sold you on him from the moment you saw him."

"I'll admit, I've always liked Thomas, but his fame and exceptional good looks have nothing to do with how I feel about him. As far as Thomas being a womanizer…well, part of that may have been your fault, dear. After Chrissie was born, you all but ignored him. He's in the public eye and just maybe you didn't give him enough attention. But that's neither here nor there, except for the fact that when and if you marry James McMann, you will need to consult Thomas."

"Of course. Why would I hide it? Thomas should be happy for me. After all, our daughter will have a wonderful home to live in, plus a stepbrother. Bobby's mother died in an accident and I intend to adopt him. I thought you would be happy for me, Mother."

"You're not wildly in love with him like you were with Thomas, nor are you afraid to live alone."

"No. I'm not afraid to live alone, nor do I feel about him like I did Thomas. But I do love him in a different sort of way, and I'm hugely attracted to him."

"Lust, dear."

"For one, yes, but I believe he would be a loyal husband. That's important to me."

"That is a point. It's clear that he's crazy about you."

Evelyn poured a healthy amount of honey on the sopapilla the waiter had just set down in front of her, and took a bite. Honey dripped through her shaking fingers and onto the tablecloth. She wiped her sticky hands on the napkin and took a drink of water. Swallowing wrong, she choked. She was angry with her mother and wanted to leave, but she didn't want to create a scene. Thomas was famous and had always treated her mother like a queen, clinging to every word she said. James hadn't. His attention had been focused upon her.

Katherine leaned toward Evelyn over the dinner table and said in a low voice, "You mentioned Mr. McMann's first wife was killed in an accident. Just what kind?" Her hazel eyes were serious. Her manner reflected suspicious thoughts.

"It was a traffic accident. She was struck by a car while crossing the street," Evelyn said, suspecting her mother was trying to make something more of it than what it was.

"Hmmm. Was she pregnant with another child?"

"I don't know. Where are you going with this?"

"Nowhere actually. Was he with her when it happened?"

"Yes, but he doesn't like to talk about it," Evelyn said.

"Still, I think you should know exactly what happened."

"Maybe. I'll see what I can find out. You don't like James, do you?"

"If I truly felt James was a good man, I would be happy for you. I have no doubt you have strong feelings for him. The truth is, dear, I have a bad feeling about this man. I wish you would wait. I think you might see some things you don't want to have in your life, or in Chrissie's. You said he was just a social drinker. How do you know?"

Evelyn sighed. "Mother, he's under a lot of pressure. He works hard. So he has a few too many after a hard day. I haven't seen him actually drunk more than four or five times. Mostly, he drinks socially."

"You've actually seen him drunk four or five times in four months? Oh, my dear. If he does have a drinking problem, he may be an alcoholic and, whether you know it or not, alcoholism is a disease."

"James goes to a support group. He won't let his social drinking get out of hand. He has everything under control," Evelyn said.

"If he goes to a support group, he obviously has had a serious problem, but at least he has sought help. That's admirable. But he shouldn't be drinking at all, not if he's an alcoholic. You need to address that. It would be best if you don't drink while you are with him. It's too tempting for him."

"How do you know so much about this, Mother?"

"Oh, darling, you know I was married once before I met your father. He was an alcoholic and quite abusive when he was drinking. I would not like to see you live the kind of life I did," Katherine said.

Evelyn's anger eased. She wished her mother had shared this part of her life with her before. It would have explained the stance she'd always taken with her family. No one was to be served more than one cocktail at happy hour and no more than two glasses of wine or beer at dinner. "I didn't know your first husband was an alcoholic or that he had been abusive. You must have been miserable."

"I was. His addiction to alcohol eroded the very fabric of our lives. I dreaded coming home after work, never knowing what sort of state I would find him in. I don't want to see you make the same mistake."

Perhaps she's right.

"Mom, I know you're concerned about me. I'll think about it."

"Good."

That evening, Evelyn wore a black silk dress that clung to her slim figure. She had chosen it to fit her somber mood.

During dinner, she was quiet, dreading the moment she had chosen to break their engagement. Now, she wasn't sure she could do it. He leaned over and kissed her on her neck, just below her gold earring, a place that never failed to arouse her. "I've ordered Champagne, a bottle of their finest, in celebration of our engagement."

Evelyn ran her fingers through her hair, brushing it back from her face. She didn't want to break their betrothal. He'd been so kind and generous with her. She didn't want to hurt him. But, she felt they needed to wait, just as her mother had said. She glanced at the ring he'd given her.

Her stomach churned. Her finger itched and had blackened where the ring fit, like she was having an allergic reaction. Was her body warning her? Thomas's grandmother, who possessed psychic abilities, would have said it was.

"We need to talk about our engagement. Perhaps you should cancel the Champagne," Evelyn said.

"Is there something wrong? I thought you liked Champagne," James said.

"It's not that." She cleared her throat and said, "It's us. We haven't known each other long enough to be engaged. I need more time."

"Evelyn, we have so much together. We are so compatible. Why would you say that you need more time? I miss you so much when we're apart. You know how much I love both you and Chrissie. Have you begun to question your love for me?"

"No. I just think we should wait a little longer before we marry," she said, squirming in her chair.

"Why do you want to wait?" He was in a hurry to make their relationship permanent. He was afraid she would find out about his illness, that he needed to take his medication every day in order to be normal. He was schizoaffective, and without it, he was a danger to everyone.

"You did say you would give me time to decide."

"And I have. It's been nearly a month."

"Still, I would like more time."

He straightened in his chair, pulled back, and looked directly into her eyes. "You had lunch with your mother today. Was this her idea?"

She nodded.

"She's being overly protective of you, interfering

where she shouldn't."

"She means well," Evelyn said.

"No one can know our relationship but us," James said, taking her hand in his.

"I know. You are convincing and compelling."

He grinned. "What does your heart tell you? Do you really want to wait? I have three weeks of vacation coming up. We'll fly to Hawaii, marry on the garden island of Kauai. You mentioned you would love to see Australia. We'll go there for our honeymoon. Chrissie will be with her father. It's a perfect time for us, don't you think?" James asked.

The waiter came with the Champagne and poured two glasses, giving Evelyn a moment to think. It seemed perfect. What about the reading she had had in Sedona? Had Running Deer been referring to James or Thomas? Thomas had already hurt her. He had deceived her and nothing had been as she had expected after that. Running Deer must have been referring to Thomas and to her past.

"To us," James said, toasting. His blue-green eyes had a twinkle in them as they met hers.

"To us," Evelyn said.

The next weekend, they flew to Hawaii and were married on Kauai in the Fern Grotto. She'd had a few moments before she said "I do" when she'd nearly bolted. But James's partners had flown in from Florida, Vince and his wife Danielle, and Sal with his special lady of the moment.

She'd shrugged her fear off to the institution of marriage itself. The thought of marrying again had frightened her so much she hadn't been able to spell the word, not since her divorce from Thomas. She wanted her second marriage to last forever. James was different than

Thomas. She didn't think that he wouldn't ever deceive her with other women. She was sorry none of her family had been there, not even her sister Lainey.

They spent Christmas in their condo on Hanalei along with Vince, Danielle, Sal, and his girlfriend. Christmas day was a mix of joy and sadness. She missed Chrissie, her mom and dad, and even Thomas. On the other hand, she was happy to be with James and her new friends in a land she loved. But, when she went to bed alone that night, she tossed and turned, wondering what Chrissie and Thomas had done for Christmas. For the first time since they'd left for the Islands, James had too much to drink and had passed out on the floor near the Christmas tree. She'd expected an incredible night of lovemaking.

CHAPTER 8

Thomas knew his stage performance hadn't been up to par that evening. If it hadn't been for his surprise guest, a gorgeous superstar in her own right, the opening at the fabulous new casino New Year's Eve would have been a flop.

"What was wrong last night, darlin'?" Julie asked.

"I had a call late this afternoon. It was from Evelyn, Chrissie's mother...my ex-wife."

"And?

"She's married again, to a developer from Florida."

"Why should that bother you?" Julie asked.

He sighed. "Evelyn and I share split custody of Chrissie. She should have had the courtesy of telling me beforehand, at least."

"What do you know about this man?"

"I know Chrissie doesn't like him. Neither does Evelyn's mother," Thomas said in a worried tone.

"Why doesn't Evelyn's mother like him?"

"She believes he is an alcoholic."

Julie drew her narrow, arched brows together. "I should hope he isn't."

"I can't imagine Evelyn being with an alcoholic,"

Thomas said. "She's practically a teetotaler."

"I haven't met her, but it's possible she just didn't see him clearly. You know what they say, love is blind. Actually, I think it's chemistry that blinds us."

"You mean lust, Julie," Thomas said.

She nodded, gazed into his eyes, and smiled. Her warm, chocolate brown eyes twinkled. "I believe I've been blinded before, but not this time. Why doesn't Chrissie like him?"

"She says he has bad vibes and calls him Mr. Stranger Danger."

Julie laughed. "That sounds like your grandmother talking, Thomas."

"It does," he said, laughing. He sighed. "I hate to say this, but I'd bet a thousand to one that Evelyn's gotten herself into one sorry mess."

"You still love her, don't you, Thomas?"

"Yes. I think I always will. I was hoping maybe we would get back together. I think I would have had a chance, if she just would have let me explain."

"As I remember, there were rumors flying, rumors about you and your agent."

He nodded. "There were. She was a good friend, attractive too. We were together a lot. The tabloids latched onto that and wouldn't let go. There was nothing going on…just a nice friendship and a good working relationship."

"Like us."

"Exactly. You are planning on staying here, in the guest room, while you're in Vegas, aren't you?"

"I really shouldn't. Your daughter is here. You need to spend your time with her, and I need to rehearse."

"Chrissie loves you. She asked if you were coming.

There's plenty of room. You know I have a grand piano. Bring in your pianist. He can stay here, too. I'm one of the few who know your secret. I'll give you and Brad the guest suite."

"How did you know? We've been trying to keep our affair a secret."

"I've known you for a long time, Julie. It wasn't hard to guess."

"As long as the tabloids don't guess."

"Be careful and they won't."

Chrissie ran into the room. "Julie! I didn't know you were here. Why didn't you tell me, Daddy?"

Thomas grinned. "Because, pumpkin, she just arrived yesterday."

"You're going to stay with us, aren't you, Julie?" Chrissie asked.

Julie smiled and said, "I'm thinking about it."

"You can stay in my room with me," Chrissie said.

"Thank you, darlin'. That's very generous of you."

"I've offered her our best guest room. I hope she'll take me up on it," Thomas said.

"Please, Julie," Chrissie said, begging.

"All right then. I'd love to, but only if I can teach you my new duet."

Chrissie beamed. "With a dance too, like before?"

"Yes, sugar. With a dance too, a new dance," Julie said.

"You're going to turn my daughter into a superstar yet." Thomas groaned.

"Would you like to hear the music?"

"Yes! Do you mind, Daddy?"

"Not at all. Go ahead, you two. I have something else to do right now anyway," Thomas said.

Once he had a moment to himself, his mind traveled to Evelyn. He wondered if the man she'd married would bring her the happiness she deserved. He didn't think so. The very thought of her with someone else tore him apart. If only he'd been able to talk to her, explain that he'd never been unfaithful to her. He knew she'd loved him. Damn the tabloids and the gossip.

CHAPTER 9

Evelyn reminisced. With the exception of Christmas Day and James's performance as a lover, their honeymoon had been a dream. He'd presented his marriage gift to her on the flight over to Australia. When he handed her an envelope, she hadn't thought he would give her a wedding gift. She'd thought perhaps he'd decided to give her shopping money.

Opening it, she found the deed to the villa in Paradise Valley made out in her name only.

The note he'd written had said, *"For you, my darling Evelyn. In case something happens to me, you will always have a home, one near those you love. No matter what time brings, remember how much I love you."*

She'd been puzzled, but had thanked him for such a generous gift, one she'd never expected. She began to wonder if he was ill and hadn't told her. She remembered the nightmare she'd had the night before she'd met him. She'd met a handsome stranger resembling James whose face had transformed into something hideous. Later, when they were home, in Florida, she would ask if he had any health problems.

After they'd settled into their hotel in Sydney, they'd

toured Australia's oldest settlement. Set on the shores of Port Jackson, Sydney was a thriving, spectacular city. She'd insisted upon visiting the Sydney Opera House, where they took photos with the Sydney Harbor Bridge in the background.

For most of his life, James had wanted to visit Australia, especially the outback. After they'd left Sydney, they'd traveled to Ayers Rock and nearby Kata Tjuta where they had found impressive monoliths. A hiker, Evelyn had insisted upon walking the 6km circuit.

Though he didn't like to hike, he'd amiably agreed.

From there, they'd moved onto Perth, the capital of Western Australia. Set on the Swan and Canning Rivers, the Indian Ocean was to the west, the Darling Ranges to the East. They both fell in love with Perth and its magnificent beaches.

By the end of their third week in the vibrant country, James became irritable. He paced back and forth and began talking to himself. On the long plane ride back home, he drank until the hostess refused to serve him. He reeked of gin and snored while he slept. A bother to everyone around him, they moved to other seats that were empty. Evelyn tried her best to stay seated near him, but finally moved to another seat too.

When they returned to Boca Raton with Chrissie, he continued his heavy drinking. Evelyn was sick of it. Her mother had been right. She knew she needed to approach him with the problem.

"I didn't know you were such a heavy drinker, James. Is something wrong?"

"No. Nothing's wrong. I enjoy having a few drinks. Why not have a drink with me?"

"You know I never drink during the day. It makes me

sleepy," Evelyn said.

He laughed. "That's not much of an excuse. You can always take a nap with me, like we did in Australia. Or I could even hang a couple of hammocks on the terrace. Remember our trip to Mexico?"

She nodded. "Those were memorable times. We'll do it again, but today, I'd really like to finish my research for the novel I'm planning to write."

He shook his head. "You spend way too much time writing as it is. And for what? I don't see you making much money with your articles. You might find it more rewarding if you stopped that foolishness and enrolled in cooking classes."

"Foolishness? Writing to me is not foolishness. I love it. Did you say cooking classes?" Evelyn asked, aghast. She'd always hated cooking. She could do it, and do it well, but she felt there were other things more worthwhile to do. Anyone could prepare a decent meal. Or for that matter, if they couldn't, go to a restaurant.

"Cooking can be very creative. I would like it very much if you would do that," James said.

"I don't believe I'm hearing this. You knew from the very beginning I was a writer," Evelyn said.

"Yes, but I thought it was a hobby," James said, knowing full well that it wasn't.

"A hobby. You mean like learning about fine wines?" Evelyn asked, raising her voice.

He grinned. "Now that would be enjoyable. That's another thing you could do. By the way, we're not having another vegetarian dinner tonight, are we? I'm sick of vegetarian dishes and seafood. I'll pick up some steaks and we can barbecue them. Do we have any red wine?"

Evelyn was more than irritated. James had pushed her

buttons and there was nothing amusing about their conversation, even though James seemed to be enjoying it. Funny, it was as though he'd been planning it for months.

He'd gained weight since she'd met him. He had love handles and was beginning to have a paunch. With his weight gain, his sex drive disappeared. Drunk or sober, he was all but impotent.

"We have a couple of my favorite wines."

"What are they?" James asked.

"Two bottles each of The Fat Bastard—Shiraz, and Merlot," Evelyn said, grinning.

"The Fat Bastard? I hope you're not referring to me. I know I've gained weight."

"Actually, that's really the brand name. It's an imported wine from France. Fat Bastard is a British expression describing a rich and full wine. It's made from the very best vineyards north of Nimes in the Languedoc Roussillon region of Southern France."

"Sorry. I guess you do know something about wines. I thought you were insulting me," James said.

She shook her head. "No, I wasn't. I don't like to insult people, nor do I like to argue. It's just not worth it, unless it is to uphold my principles."

"Good. Then I can count on you to stop writing and begin a creative cooking class," he said.

"No. You have misunderstood me. I want you to know that writing to me is not a hobby. I don't intend to give it up. In fact, I am going to begin my first novel soon. But, I will choose to concentrate on that area of my life when you aren't home. In the meantime, I'll look into some gourmet cooking classes. That way, we both win. Sound fair?"

"We'll see," James said.

"There is one thing I would really like you to do for me, though."

"What's that?"

"Please attend your support meetings and stop drinking."

"Shut up, Steve," James murmured.

She shook her head, went to the coat closet, and put on her windbreaker. "I'm going for a walk on the beach."

By the time she came back, James reeked of whiskey and had passed out in one of the recliners in front of the oversized TV.

She hated what her life had become and wished she'd never married him. The following day was a repeat.

"James, you're sick. You must begin going to your meetings and stop drinking. I cannot live like this," Evelyn said, knowing that she was threatening him.

"What's happened to you, Evelyn? You used to be fun. Now that we're married, you've turned into a nag and a bitch. I'm going to have a drink now. A Bloody Mary. Have one with me. It won't hurt you."

"You're right. One or two drinks won't hurt me. But it will you. You're an alcoholic, James. You can't have just one drink. I don't want to encourage you."

"You've been attending that damned support group for families and friends of alcoholics, haven't you?" James asked.

"Yes. I have."

"I thought so. Don't go back. They're idiots…worse than alcoholics. They're co-dependents, a really sick bunch. You shouldn't be around them. They're giving you bad ideas. Why did you go to a meeting anyway?"

"Because I was miserable. I knew when I met you, you were a social drinker, but I didn't think you were an alcoholic. You seemed to be okay in Mexico and afterwards when we took Chrissie to Disney. But after we were married, your sobriety didn't last long," Evelyn said, her eyes beginning to tear.

"Steve was right. You're beginning to sound and act just like Elaine."

"You really had me fooled, James. Before I married you, you were charming. But now, all of that charm has vanished. You're drunk the majority of the time. You're bossy, rude, and disgusting. Your temper's short; your manners are foul. I can't believe you are the same person."

"Shut, up, Evelyn, before you really make me mad," James said, ignoring the fact that tears were rolling down her cheeks.

She shook her head. He'd proven to be a sorry excuse for a husband or even a friend. How could his partners tolerate him?

"Mommy," Chrissie said, running into the living room.

"Yes, darling," Evelyn said, wiping a tear from her cheek.

Chrissie frowned. "Are you okay, Mommy?"

"Yes," she said, glancing at her watch. "It's time to go to your piano lesson, isn't it?"

"Mmmhmm. Will you take me?"

"Yes, of course. Excuse me, James. I need to leave now."

"Then go," he said coldly.

"Mommy, I don't like James" she said when they were out of earshot.

Neither do I.

"He smells sour and he's mean to me. He's always telling me to leave the room, to go to bed. I want to see my real daddy."

So do I. But I'm determined to give this marriage a good try.

"Give James a chance, Chrissie. He's not accustomed to having us around," Evelyn said.

"He doesn't pay attention to his own son when he visits either. That's mean. I like Bobby. He doesn't have a mommy like I do. He told me he wished you were his real mother. He's afraid you will leave his dad and he'll never see you again," Chrissie said.

Evelyn sighed. "It's too bad Bobby doesn't have a better home life. If James changes his ways, I'd like to adopt him."

"Bobby would like that. So would I, except I don't like James."

"I'm sure this is just a temporary period of adjustment, Chrissie. I hope he'll return to being the man he was when I first met him."

"I didn't like him then either," Chrissie said.

Evelyn sighed again. Maybe she should send her back to Thomas, at least for a while. She didn't like Chrissie being around a drunk, and she was right about Bobby. James all but ignored his son. She felt badly for him. He'd only been a baby when his mother had been killed. He was fifteen years old now and enrolled in Admiral Farragut Academy, a fine military school in St. Petersburg, Florida. His manners were impeccable, but he was hungry for love and attention. If only James would stop drinking.

He'd stopped attending his support group months ago. When no one would drink with him, he drank alone and fell into a deep depression. He paced back and forth across the living room, talked to himself and to Steve, who seemed to be an imaginary character. None of the household employees or Evelyn had ever met Steve. His behavior was filled with paranoia. They had a state-of-the-art alarm system, but on top of that, he installed double locks on the doors and another outdoor camera.

James hated pets, but surrendered to purchasing a German shepherd puppy. His intention was to train the shepherd to protect him from those he believed wished him harm. He named him Terminator. Evelyn was uneasy, not because of the puppy, but because of James's intent. He was paranoid about many things, imagined things. One night, he'd dressed in black jeans and a black tee and hid behind a large bush by their bedroom window watching both the window and the front door. She wondered if he or the business had been receiving threats. But, when she mentioned it to Vince, he'd told her no, they were not being threatened.

She knew James cared no more for Chrissie than she cared for him. Now that she wasn't getting along well with James, his blue-green eyes often stared out at Chrissie in his drunken states with contempt and murderous rage.

In spite of James's training, everyone in the household loved the puppy, especially Chrissie. She named him Tor. Treated well by everyone but James, he was a friendly, happy dog except to his owner. When he was drunk, James kicked him, locked him in the garage, and didn't feed him. Evelyn and Chrissie let him out, fed him, took him for walks, and played with him. She wished for the talented, charming, handsome man James had been when she'd met him. She'd never loved him as she had Thomas, but she did love him. He was certainly worth saving.

Evelyn decided the only way that would be possible was if he sought counseling from a professional who could treat not only his alcoholism, but speak to him about his imaginary character. In fact, she herself could use a counselor to help her deal with his apparent problems.

She called a psychiatrist she had met recently at a book signing. When she'd made the appointments, she felt so much better. It was past time she started her new book.

CHAPTER 10

James awoke with a splitting headache and a taste in his mouth like a dirty washcloth. The voices were back and not even the booze could keep them away. Evelyn didn't understand.

He couldn't tell her. He was afraid she would leave him if she knew he was crazy. He sighed. They weren't getting along well and it was all because of him. She wasn't a bitch; he was a bastard…a fat one, just like the bottle had said.

He had gained weight. He'd been drinking too much and hadn't taken his walks or worked out at the gym. He hadn't ridden his bike or done his regular laps in the pool. Their sex life was practically non-existent. When he was drunk, she pushed him away. When he was on his meds, he lost his desire. He was afraid she would look elsewhere. Sal's attraction to Evelyn was obvious. Sal was a handsome man, better looking than he was. It was a no-win situation.

The continual hallucinations and voices were driving him crazy. Meditation wasn't helping anymore. He needed to call the doctor before did something he might regret. He'd told him not to marry, not until he'd been sober for at least six months and his mental illness had been stabilized by medication. He hadn't listened. Pulling on his jogging shorts, he decided to call him after he went for a run.

When he came back and had showered, Evelyn made his breakfast, but was extraordinarily quiet. Oh man! He must have said or done something to her that he couldn't remember.

"You're quiet this morning, Evelyn. Is something wrong?" James asked.

"Nothing I want to mention right now," Evelyn said.

"Have I had any telephone calls from Vin or Sal?"

"Not that I know of."

"She's lying. Sal stopped by," Steve whispered in his ear.

"Come on, Steve. She'd tell me if he had," James said softly.

He laughed. *"No, she wouldn't,"* Steve said, whispering again.

"Who are you talking to? There's no one in this room but us, James," Evelyn said.

"You're sure Sal didn't stop by this morning?" James asked, ignoring her question.

"If he did, I must have been in the shower and not heard the doorbell. And there is no one else in this room. You need to see a doctor, James. You're hearing voices and hallucinating."

"He was in the shower with her, dummy. Remember the shower you wanted to take with Evelyn in Mexico? That's the kind of shower they were taking. Sal was screwing her in the shower, dummy, just like he did with Elaine."

"I am not hallucinating or hearing imaginary voices. You know who Steve is," James said.

"What? I've never met Steve and I haven't seen Sal

since your last meeting here," Evelyn said.

"You're lying. I hope you're not having an affair. I won't tolerate that."

Evelyn sighed and shook her head in disgust. "You needn't worry about that. I would never consider such a thing. Even thinking it is an insult to both me and to Sal."

"It's meant as a warning."

"A warning? What do you mean?" Evelyn asked, alarmed.

His lips tightened. He looked at her sharply. "I warned Elaine, and the other one. Unfortunately, neither took me seriously."

Evelyn drew her brows together. "Neither? Have you been married twice before me? What are you trying to tell me?"

"My first wife had lovers. In fact, I'm not even sure Bobby's mine," James said.

"That's ridiculous. He looks just like you. You aren't accusing me of taking a lover, are you?"

"Just fair warning. I've noticed you stay as far away as you can from me in bed. I know you aren't frigid. I can only think of one thing that would account for that."

"Oh? And what do you think that might be?" Evelyn asked in a tone that could freeze a waterfall on a hot day.

"That you're having an affair."

She shook her head. "Did you ever consider that it might be your addiction to alcohol that turns me off? You should have told me you were an alcoholic before we married."

"You're beginning to sound just like Elaine. You knew I had a few drinks now and then."

"Now and then? How about a constant now?"

James turned in his chair, grabbed her, and shook her.

The voices screamed in his ears. *"Shut her up! Get rid of her."* He could barely contain himself. He glanced to the counter. A steak knife lay on the counter. His first thought was to grab it and tear into her. He rose from the chair. Halfway to the counter, he turned and said, "Enough, Evelyn. I'm your husband. Show me a little respect, for heaven's sake. You don't lack for anything. Why I've even taken on your little brat. I doubt you'd find many men that would raise another man's child."

"Are you calling my little girl a little brat?" Evelyn asked coldly. In that moment, if there was a shred of affection left for James, it evaporated.

James straightened his tall frame and struggled to keep the voices at bay. He hated Chrissie. She took too much of Evelyn's attention from him, plus she'd never liked him. They'd be better off if she weren't there. He blurted out, "She is a brat, Evelyn. She won't mind me. This morning, when I was reading the paper, I asked her to get something for me. She refused and told me I wasn't her real daddy."

"What did you ask her to do?"

"I'd left my morning eye opener on the terrace. I asked her to carry it in for me," James said.

"You mean your Bloody Mary?"

"Bloody Mary, tomato juice, what does it matter?"

"I do believe that is enough of this conversation, James. I'll see that you're not bothered by Chrissie again." Evelyn turned and marched out of the room. As soon as she found a private moment, she called Thomas.

"Thomas. This is Evelyn."

Thomas chuckled. "I know who it is, sweetie. Weren't you my wife for four years?"

"Yes."

"What's up? I can tell by the tone of your voice something is wrong."

She took a deep breath, hating to tell Thomas that yes, something was terribly wrong in her new marriage. "Sadly, Mother was right. I should have waited before I married James."

"Has he hurt you? Or Chrissie?"

Evelyn was silent for a long moment. "He's an alcoholic, Thomas. He stopped going to his support group weeks after we were married. But I think there's something else wrong, too."

"What's that?"

"He talks to someone named Steve, an imaginary person, I think. He just threatened me. He believes I've been having an affair. I'm not, of course. But worse than that, he called Chrissie a brat and she despises him."

"Sounds like you're in a dangerous relationship, at the very least. Why are you staying with him? Leave before someone's hurt. File a divorce here in Las Vegas. I'll find a nice villa for you and Chrissie," Thomas said.

"I don't know. I wasn't thinking of leaving him, at least not at this early date. Maybe if he goes back to his support group or sees a counsellor, he will be all right."

"Then at least send Chrissie to me. Don't take long to make up your mind yourself, Evelyn. I know you're not the sort of person that would have an affair. And speaking of affairs, we need to talk. You misjudged me, took things at face value. Promise me that talk soon."

Evelyn hesitated. She didn't want to discuss old matters, namely their divorce. Still, maybe she owed him that. She probably should have done it long before now. What would it hurt? "All right."

"Good. Now, put Chrissie on a plane as soon as

possible…today. Call me just as soon as you have reservations. I'll pay for her ticket."

"Thank you, Thomas. But, there's no problem with money. I have plenty in my account. I need to call for reservations and do this while James is out."

"My God, you're afraid of him. Don't let him know that."

Evelyn had heard the trace of fear in Thomas's voice. Shuddering, she said, "I won't. Goodbye. Thank you again."

Fearing for Chrissie's well-being, Evelyn had her on a plane for Las Vegas by evening.

CHAPTER 11

It was late September when they held the barbecue and beach party to celebrate the day they'd met. Delayed due to Hurricanes Charley, Frances, and Ivan, the celebration was nearly a month late. Many of guests had flown in from the hurricane stricken areas. Some had lost their homes and taken temporary quarters while their own were being repaired. Some had chosen to move to inland states. Hot and sultry, the breeze from the warm waters of the Atlantic couldn't cool them off. Tempers were running as hot as the weather.

That evening, Hurricane Jeanne, a Cape Verde storm that had already inundated the Dominican Republic, Puerto Rico, and Haiti was reported to be headed toward the northern Bahamas. A category 2 storm, projections indicated it would head toward Florida, possibly striking the coast on Sunday. But the weather bureau had missed on Charley. It didn't strike Tampa Bay, but instead strengthened and wiped out much of Punta Gorda, Charlotte Harbor, and inland areas like Arcadia. Within James's circle, no one really believed Jeanne would strike the coast within the next day or so and, like Andrew, no one expected Jeanne to become a killer hurricane. It was unthinkable that Florida could be hit by five named storms in one year.

Not a soul thought of turning on the TV to listen to the weather forecast. The out-of-towners were flying home in the morning anyway. Beer, wine, and cocktails were flowing freely.

Women were laughing, flirting dangerously, and gossiping. Once the men had their fill of the barbecue and beer, they retreated to the library for a few games of poker. Evelyn was anxious for the guests to leave, for the men to stop drinking and gambling. She was concerned about James. Knowing the temptation would be too great with all of the other men drinking, she was certain he would over indulge. She drew her brows together. He was abusive, mentally and physically, when he was drinking. She had a bad feeling that tonight would be a night like no other.

She excused herself from her guests and moved into the kitchen, wanting a few minutes alone. Vivian, Evelyn's best friend and Dr. Sam's wife, followed her into the kitchen. When Mae, the housekeeper, left the room, she said, "I hope you won't think I'm interfering, but both Samuel and I have noticed James hasn't been looking well. His eyes and skin have a yellowish tint, a sign he may have suffered damage to his liver. He needs to come in for a physical."

"I've noticed the same. It breaks my heart to see him like this," Evelyn said.

"If he keeps drinking at the same rate he has been, I'm afraid the alcohol damage to his system will lead to cirrhosis of the liver."

Evelyn sighed. "That can lead to liver cancer, can't it?"

"Yes. The end result is usually a painful death."

"I was afraid of that. That's the reason I've suggested to James that he see Dr. Sam, his regular doctor, for a physical. I've been urging him to go to a support group again and see the Psychiatrist that I made an appointment with. But he just becomes angry with me when I suggest it. He says everyone at the support group is a loser."

"Well then, maybe Samuel needs to have a serious talk with James. Next week, his receptionist will give him a call and remind him that he needs to book an appointment for his annual physical."

"That would be wonderful. I hope his receptionist doesn't forget to put James on her list of calls," Evelyn said.

Vivian laughed and said, "Oh, she won't. I've been filling in while his receptionist is away."

"Good. Maybe it's just what he needs."

"It's important that he come in. If not, Samuel may call Vince and Sal. Since they are his partners, they need to be aware of just how serious this is. Maybe they can have a talk with James about his drinking. I expect he's an embarrassment to them at the very least."

Evelyn nodded. *I'm sure he is. If they've ever had to have the busboys pick James up off the floor of a restaurant and carry him to his car as many times as I have, they would be his ex-partners by now.*

"James's first wife, Elaine, was terribly worried about him," Vivian said.

"Were you friends?"

"Yes. You remind me of her. She was a lovely person."

"It was too bad about her accident."

Vivian nodded. "Yes, Both Elaine's and Clarissa's."

"He's never mentioned her to me. Who is Clarissa? What happened?"

"Clarissa was a fiancée' of James's. She was killed in an accident, a boating accident."

Evelyn sucked in her breath. *A lot of accidents.*

"Be careful, Evelyn. Stay away from James when he's drinking. Please don't mention that I warned you. But I do like you, just as I did Elaine and Clarissa."

"Thank you for telling me, and for your concern, Vivian. Let's go back into the living room. The men should be out soon."

Enjoying their dessert, the women chatted easily among themselves about their children, social events, and designer clothing. Evelyn noticed a few of the wives seemed particularly restless and didn't seem to be listening to the conversations. She wondered if their husbands had the same problem James did.

"It's about time our husbands were finished with the game, don't you think, Evelyn?" Danielle asked. "Vince will be lucky to have a cent left to his name."

"They've been in there a long time."

"Long enough for the stakes to have been extraordinarily high. Some of us will need to drive our husbands home, I'm afraid."

Evelyn drew her brows together. If the stakes had been high and James had lost, he would be insufferable. Lightning streaked across the sky, lighting up the living room. Thunder rumbled ominously, almost like a foreboding scene in a movie.

The door to the study opened. The men spilled out, mostly laughing, though a few, like James, wore sour expressions. With a glance, Evelyn knew the stakes had been high. James had lost. The gin bottle would be empty tomorrow. The guests didn't linger long, except for Vince.

Staying on, he asked Vivian and Samuel to take

Danielle home. He said he had something to discuss with James.

Exhausted, Evelyn went to bed. Sleeping fitfully, she was rudely awakened by a glass crashing to the floor, the sickly sweet smell of gin, and the sound of James's voice. He yanked her out of bed. Shaking her, he asked, "Do you think I don't know what you were doing on the beach while I was meeting with Vince?"

"Wh-what are you talking about?" Evelyn asked, fully awake now.

"I know you've been having an affair. You just waited until the guests had left, all except for Vince and Sal. You were on the beach with Sal," James said loudly.

"Sal! Sal is your partner as is Vince. He left when everyone else did. Besides, I would never be unfaithful to you."

"You're lying. You're no better than Elaine was."

"You're imagining this, just like you imagined I was having an affair with the dry cleaning man last week. You could have been arrested. The housekeeper, Mae, and I both saw you, crawling around the house on your belly with a shotgun. You intended to shoot the poor man. He was terrified. He came to the front door, trembling and white as a ghost. Now, they refuse to deliver cleaning to our home. I don't blame them. You need help. Not only a medical doctor, but a psychiatrist, too."

"The hell I do. There's nothing wrong with me that a good woman and a tall gin and tonic wouldn't fix. You need to be taught a lesson. I should have done it long ago." James took her by her shoulders and shoved her across the room.

Slammed against the wall, she banged her head. He moved in on her, his fists doubled up. Evelyn shielded her face and braced for the blow that was about to come. She screamed until she was knocked down to the hardwood floors by the power of his fists hitting her again and again.

Her face hurt, her ribs, her entire body hurt. He'd beat her to death if he could. Maybe, if she let her body go slack, he would quit then. He eased up a moment to catch his breath. He turned his back for a half a second. Painfully, she rose and got up before he could hit her again. She needed a weapon.

He came at her. His face was red. He was not a small man. For a moment, Evelyn forgot all about her slender frame and small stature. She was mad now, tired of his insufferable abuse. She turned, ran, and grabbed a lamp. She swung around toward him, her arms raised, holding the lamp with both hands. She brought it down upon him with all her might. It grazed him and only served to anger him more.

"You crazy bitch! I'm gonna kill you."

He grabbed her and shoved her to the floor. He was on top of her, pulling her nightgown up with one hand while his other was around her throat, strangling her. He moved his hand from her nightgown to unzip his pants. Blood dripped down the side of his face where the lamp had grazed him.

She gasped for breath and tried to free herself. *God help me. Sex and murder are the only things on his mind and maybe not in that order.* Pinned down by his heavy body, she couldn't move. There was no way to protect herself. His eyes flashed his hatred and his lust. Thunder rumbled, shaking the house.

Pounding came at the door. Tor barked. James pulled back and released his hands. "Help! Someone help me! Call the police!" she screamed, her voice already hoarse.

The door flew open. Vince stood there with, Bobby, Mae, and Terry behind him. Tor snarled and advanced on James.

"Get away from her, James. Now. Damned good thing I forgot my jacket and had to come back. Call nine-one-one and the police, Terry," he said to the butler, who had been hired for the party.

"Get out of here, Vince," James said. "This is my business."

"Let her be, James," Vince said, moving to him.

Tor moved to Evelyn and licked her hand. James looked over his shoulder. Lightning streaked across the sky, brightening the room. His expression betrayed his innermost feelings. Madness radiated from his eyes. Vince, Terry, and Bobby pulled James away from Evelyn.

"If you want to live, get out. Don't ever come back. If you do, you'll be sorry. No wife of mine is going to act like a slut. The last one got what she was asking for," James shouted. "And so will you."

"Calm down, James. She's leaving," Vince said.

Chills moved up Evelyn's spine, spreading to every nerve and fiber of her body. A coldness settled into her bones and into her heart. Her mother had been right. Maybe right about James's first wife, too. Maybe she *had* been pushed in front of the speeding car…by James.

Who had he meant when he'd said the last one? Clarissa?

Her head pounded. Her shoulder throbbed. She had to get out of the house before something else happened. Painfully, she moved to the closet and slipped on the first sundress she could reach, along with a pair of sandals. She took a tote bag from the back of her closet and tossed in cosmetics, a couple of gowns, shorts, and t-shirts. Stuffing dresses into a garment bag, she grabbed her purse, hugged Tor, and ran out the sliding glass door onto the patio and into the tropical downpour. All she could think of was escape.

She rounded the house and thanked God that she'd parked in the driveway. Tossing her clothing into the trunk of the black Mercedes, she got into the car and headed north on A1A toward Delray and then onto Interstate 95 north to Vero Beach. She was wet, cold, shivering, nauseous, and in horrible pain.

She wasn't sure she'd make it to Lainey's. The rain was heavy. She could barely see the road. The Mercedes crawled up the highway in the storm. Going slowly, she turned on the radio to take her mind off the storm and her pain. By the time she turned off onto Hwy. 60, the Vero Beach exit, she knew she'd never make it to her sister's townhouse on Orchid Island. No one was there to help her. Her vision blurred. She drove directly to Indian River Memorial Hospital and parked in front of the emergency room door.

She slumped over the wheel and passed out. When she awoke, she was lying on a gurney in the emergency room. A doctor hovered over her. "Mrs. McMann, I need to examine you now."

"How do you know my name?"

"We checked your identification when you were brought in. Don't worry. Your handbag is safe, all its contents intact."

"The car?"

"Brenda, the nurse who will be overseeing you, moved it to the parking lot and locked it. Your keys are in your handbag."

"Thank you," Evelyn said weakly. "You didn't call my

husband, did you?"

"Not yet," the doctor said.

"Don't," Evelyn pleaded.

The doctor drew his heavy brows together. "Was he responsible for this?"

"Yes," she said, and sighed.

"Don't worry, Mrs. McMann. We'll take good care of you."

"Thank you."

"I know you're in pain. We'll relieve that as soon as I finish examining you."

The doctor took her temperature, blood pressure, poked and prodded, sent her for x-rays and gave her what they could to relieve her pain. She'd suffered a slight concussion, bruised ribs, and multiple bruises on her neck. She would need to stay overnight in the hospital.

During the night, the nurse awakened her every three hours. She was made to feel as comfortable as possible. When she awoke on Saturday, she called her sister Lainey.

"That damned Irishman! I'd like to come right down there and take care of him myself," Lainey said.

As much as it hurt, Evelyn laughed…the first laugh she'd had for months. Lainey had always had a hot temper, hot enough to match her flaming red hair.

"Don't laugh. I mean it. Now, Evie, please feel free to go to my townhouse and rest, but not too long. By that I mean you must leave tomorrow…early. There's a fierce hurricane headed your way. The last I heard, the center of the hurricane was a hundred and thirty-five miles east of Grand Abaco Island in the Bahamas. That position placed the hurricane three hundred and fifteen miles east of the Florida coast. Whether you're up to it or not, call my attorney, Greg Stuart, this afternoon. I'll call him ahead of time so he'll be expecting your call. He'll come to the townhouse to talk with you."

Evelyn exhaled a sigh of relief. "Thanks, Lainey. I'll be there just as soon as I'm released from the hospital."

"I'd like to speak with your doctor before we hang up. After that, I'm going to call the airlines and make a reservation to Phoenix for you tomorrow morning. Greg or his secretary will take you to the airport. Your flight will already be paid for, so all you will need to do is show up on time and board the plane. Mom and Dad will be waiting for you. I'll come down from Sedona later tomorrow afternoon. Maybe I'll bring Running Deer, too. I think this was the dangerous situation he was referring to."

"Probably so. As usual, you're a miracle worker. Is the hurricane really as bad as you've said?" Evelyn asked, hoping Lainey had been exaggerating.

"Good grief! It's already inundated the Dominican Republic, Puerto Rico, and Haiti as a tropical storm. It's much more that that now and gaining in strength. The last I heard, it was traveling at twelve miles per hour. I'm hoping it will slow down, stall out, and turn away from Florida."

"Me too. Oh. The doctor's waiting right here to talk with you. Thanks again, Lainey. What would I do without you?"

"Honestly, I don't know. I'll see you tomorrow evening."

After the doctor had spoken with Lainey, Evelyn was immediately released. Brenda, who had been her nurse, drove her to Lainey's townhouse on Orchid Island. She insisted upon going to the grocery for her and volunteered to stay the afternoon just in case she needed anything else.

When Brenda left, Evelyn moved to the white brocade sofa and sank into it. Deciding she would take a short nap, she kicked off her shoes, lied down, and shut her eyes. Dozing off, she was awakened by a knock at the front door. Abruptly awakened, she sat up and blinked her eyes a couple of times. Remembering where she was and who she was to meet, she rose. Making her way to the front door, she smoothed her hair and brushed it away from her face with her fingers.

Peeking through the peep hole in the door, she saw a nice-looking man of medium height who held a briefcase. "Who is it?" she asked.

"Greg. Greg Stuart, Lainey's friend."

Evelyn opened the door. "Come in, Greg. I'm Evelyn."

"Lainey's told me all about you, Evelyn. I'm very happy to meet you. I just wish it could be in more pleasant circumstances. You look like you were hurt badly. Mind if I take some photos?"

"Are you kidding? I'm not very photogenic right now."

"It'll help with the case."

"Okay. You are doing me a huge favor by taking the time to come over this afternoon. Would you like some coffee or iced tea to drink while we talk?" Evelyn asked.

"Yes, but I make great coffee. Let's go into the kitchen and I'll take care of the drinks…photos after we talk."

"Spoil me. It hurts to move. Lainey said you were nice. She was right."

He grinned. "Thanks. Are you on pain pills?"

She nodded.

"Good thing. I've always found Lainey's kitchen comfortable," Greg said as he was measuring out the coffee. Your sister said you had been married before and divorced from your first husband not long ago."

"That's right."

"What state were you divorced in?"

"Nevada."

"I expect Florida's a little different. You are a Florida resident, aren't you?"

"Yes."

"Good. If you file an uncontested divorce, it will go much quicker. Do you think your husband will contest the divorce?"

"Maybe. I hope not," Evelyn said.

"From what Lainey told me, you haven't been married long. I can see myself that he physically abused you," Greg said, placing two cups of steaming hot coffee down on the table.

"I was just released from Indian River Memorial Hospital," Evelyn said, taking a sip of coffee.

"Why do you think he might contest it?" Greg asked.

"Because I want part-time custody of my stepson, Bobby."

Greg glanced up at Evelyn, the coffee cup halfway to his lips. "This could be a problem," he said.

"I know, but he's a wonderful boy and there is something wrong with James."

"Do you think he's incompetent to raise his son?"

"Yes. He is an alcoholic and I believe mentally ill as well."

"All right then. This may take much more time than I thought it would. What about alimony or assets that you may have acquired together?"

"I don't want one cent from James. As far as property goes, he gave me a townhouse in Paradise Valley, Arizona for our wedding gift. If he wants it back, that's fine with me. All I want is out of the marriage and partial custody of Bobby."

"All right. Here's what I've done. Since you will need to file a marital separation agreement for an uncontested divorce, I've brought one with me. There will be a short hearing that you will need to attend. I know you will be vacationing in the west, but you will need to fly back for the hearing. As I understand it, you will not be returning to Highland Beach to reside in your marital home."

"No. I won't."

"Lainey has told me you would prefer to stay here in Indian River County while you are going through the divorce. Even though you will be out of town temporarily, you will need a residence in this county. I have made the papers out using this townhouse as your residence. Will that be all right?"

Evelyn smiled, somewhat amused. Once again, Lainey had taken care of the small details. "Yes, that will be fine."

"Good," Greg said, taking a sip of coffee. "Why don't you read this over and if it is all right, sign it we'll get started on this. If James does not contest the divorce, you will be signing the Dissolution of Marriage action relatively soon. Then we'll deal with the custody issue."

"All right." While she was reading the marital separation agreement, there was a knock at the front door.

"Are you expecting anyone?" Greg asked.

"Yes. Brenda, the nurse that drove me home from the hospital." She placed her hand on the table to steady herself while she rose from the chair. It hurt to move.

"Sit back down. I'll get it," Greg said.

"Thank you."

"You must be Brenda," Evelyn heard Greg say.

"Yes. And you are?"

"Greg Stuart. Please, call me Greg, and let me help you with those packages."

"Thanks."

Was she imagining it or did the temperature in the room just go up a notch or two. She could have sworn Greg's voice held a trace of admiration. She set the agreement down and turned to face them.

Their eyes were locked; both wore silly expressions. Evelyn stifled a giggle. Love at first sight from an onlooker's viewpoint.

Greg set the packages on the kitchen counter and Brenda began to unload them.

"Oh, my gosh. These are groceries," Greg said.

"Yes, there was hardly anything here," Brenda said. "I just bought enough for tonight and tomorrow morning."

"We're going to be evacuated from here soon. That's one of the reasons I came over just as soon as I could," Greg said. "Tomorrow will be too late."

"The hurricane?" Brenda asked.

Greg nodded. "Hurricane Jeanne is on its way. A hurricane warning was issued for the Florida coast from Florida City, south of Miami, to St. Augustine. A watch was issued for north of St. Augustine to Altamaha Sound, Georgia."

"Will I be able to fly out?" Evelyn asked, alarmed.

"I don't know. At some point today, Orlando International Airport will more than likely close down," Greg said.

"I have to get out. Is the hurricane that bad?" Evelyn asked. Her voice was full of fear and desperation, not so much because of the hurricane, but she was afraid James would look for her.

She could only imagine being trapped with James

during a Category 2 or 3 hurricane. "The hurricane is a bad one. It killed more than eleven hundred Haitians and about twelve hundred and fifty people are still missing. I'm going to go home, lower my hurricane shutters, and leave for Orlando. The firm keeps a corporate condo there near Lake Buena Vista. It's new and has hurricane shutters. It will be far safer than here, in Vero, or even Sebastian. If the airport in Orlando is closed by the time we get there, you can stay at the firm's condo with me, my partner, and his family. I know Lainey would like you to do that. If you need additional treatment for your injuries, I'll be able to take you to a doctor or even the hospital if necessary."

"All right. Thank you, Greg. I appreciate your help," Evelyn said, trying her best to keep her fear in check.

"What about you, Brenda?" Greg asked. "Where do you live?"

"Sebastian Highlands."

"I don't think that's going to be safe."

"I'm going to my stepbrother's home in Melbourne," Brenda said.

"He doesn't live on the beach, does he?" Greg asked.

"No. He lives in West Melbourne."

"Does he have hurricane shutters?" Evelyn asked.

"No, but I know he'll board up," Brenda said. "He already has the boards cut."

"That's good, but that may not be enough."

"What do you mean?" Brenda asked.

"When was the house built?" Greg asked.

"In nineteen seventy-four, I think," Brenda said.

"So, unless he's had a new roof put on, he doesn't have the new shingles designed to withstand winds of up to a hundred and thirty-five miles per hour." Greg said.

"No. we grew up here, in Florida. We've been in hurricanes before. We know what to do, and he has a safe room," Brenda said confidently.

"I'm still concerned about you," Greg said. "I have a feeling this is going to be a disaster for both the Treasure Coast and the Space Coast. I'd like it if you would come with Evelyn and me."

Brenda sighed. "I would like to, but we have already made our family hurricane plans."

"All right then. Evelyn, I don't want to rush you, but is there anything you need to know about the separation agreement?"

"No. I've already signed it."

"Good. It's photo time. After that, we'll roll down Lainey's hurricane shutters and go. We may not have much more time before the bands from the hurricane begin to move in."

"Guess I'll take these groceries to Craig's," Brenda said.

"Good idea. I'll take them out to the car for you after we have our photo shoot. I want one of you, too."

"Why?"

"Ah…to compare a normal woman to a seriously abused one."

Evelyn chuckled. It hurt to laugh, but she couldn't help herself.

Greg's face reddened. To cover his embarrassment up, he began taking photos.

When he'd finished, Evelyn said, "Brenda, would you write down your phone number and your brother's while I roll down the shutters? Oh, and your address, too. I'll give you a call from Phoenix," Evelyn said.

She nodded.

"If you don't mind, Brenda, I'd like to have those numbers, too. I'll call after the hurricane passes and see how everything went. Let me know if you need help," he said, handing her his card.

****

Late Saturday afternoon, the flight Evelyn was supposed to arrive on landed on the runway at Phoenix International Airport. William, Katherine, and Lainey waited until the last passenger departed the plane. Evelyn was not on it. Orlando International had closed down. No one had heard from her. Lines were down all over Florida from high winds. They returned home, turned on the news, then switched to the Weather Channel.

From Evelyn's parents' home in Paradise Valley, Lainey, Katherine, and William watched in horror. On September 25th, approximately 11:50 p.m., the eye of the hurricane made landfall near the southern end of Hutchinson Island, just a short distance from where Lainey's townhouse was.

"The hurricane's eye went ashore just twenty miles south of where my townhouse is. It struck as a Category Three. She may be in an evacuation center. Or, maybe she's with Greg. I know his firm has a condo in Orlando," Lainey said. "And I hope there's something left of my condo."

"I hope to God Evie wasn't in the condo," William said.

"She would have been evacuated," Lainey said.

"Listen. They are saying the highest storm surge occurred over southern Brevard, Indian River, St. Lucie, and Martin Counties."

"The highest winds of a hurricane are in the northeast quarter," William said.

"Which means Vero Beach, Sebastian, and Melbourne are receiving winds much higher than what is being reported in Ft. Pierce," Lainey said. "We can only hope Evie's safe with Greg in Orlando."

"There's no way of knowing. Telephone lines and power lines are out all over Florida. Orlando and Melbourne airports are now closed," Katherine said.

"I just can't believe this," Laniey said. "This is the fourth hurricane to hit Florida in six weeks. If I didn't know better, I'd think one of our enemies has learned to control the weather and is zeroing in on Florida. Truly, these storms have been weapons of mass destruction."

William laughed. "If that were so, wouldn't they have struck airbases or the Cape?"

"Jeanne is following the same path that Frances did. Who knows where she will go now? Her highest winds are now striking Melbourne…close to the Cape. Charley was supposed to strike Tampa Bay where McDill Air Force Base is," Lainey said.

"I didn't think about that. You might not be far off," William said.

Evelyn didn't call. Neither did Greg. No one slept that night. The following day, after the hurricane had done its horrific damage, Red Cross volunteers, FEMA, and FPL workers flooded into the badly damaged coast. Photos of the devastated area were flashed on TV and posted to sites on the Internet.

"I wish Evelyn or Greg would call," Katherine said.

"I doubt they can," William said.

"I've already called Greg's numbers. All phones are out," Lainey said in a worried tone.

"There's nothing we can do but wait for news," William said.

CHAPTER 12

"William, could you get the door? We weren't expecting anyone, were we?" Katherine asked.

"Not that I know of."

William came back into the room with a wide grin on his face and Chrissie in his arms. "We have two very welcome guests. Come on in, Thomas."

"Thanks, William. Have you heard from Evie?"

"Not a word. All communication lines are out," William said.

"It's been three days since the hurricane passed over Vero Beach," Thomas said.

"I know. We're worried sick. Power lines are down as well as phone lines. Mail is not being delivered in areas hardest hit. Some of the post offices were badly damaged. I don't know where she spent the night of the hurricane," William said.

"Damn James," Thomas said, running his hands through his dark, wavy hair.

"If it's any consolation, she wasn't with him," William said.

"No. He beat her within an inch of her life," Thomas said, clenching his fists. "I just wish I could get my hands on that animal."

"I'm right there with you, son," William said. "The thing is, I think he's a very sick man and needs treatment. I doubt this is the first time he's abused a woman."

The phone rang, interrupting their conversation.

"Excuse me," Katherine said. "I need to get the phone." Back in a moment, Katherine said, "It's Evie on the line. She's here, at Sky Harbor International Airport. She said she will take a cab home."

"No way. Tell her we're leaving now. Find out what flight she flew in on. We'll pick her up at baggage claim," Thomas said.

"Am I going to get to see Mommy now?" Chrissie asked, running into the kitchen.

"Soon. Why don't you and Chrissie pick her up, Thomas? Katherine and I need to go to the store," William said.

"Are you sure? We flew over from Vegas and I rented an SUV. There's room for all of us."

"Go ahead. We have some things to do here," he said, winking at Katherine.

"Lainey, would you like to go with us?"

"No thanks, Thomas. Actually, I'd like to take a shower and change clothes before Evelyn arrives," Lainey said.

****

Evelyn was waiting in the baggage claim with one small bag and a cosmetic bag. Her hazel eyes lit with recognition and she wore a brilliant smile.

"Thomas! I didn't expect you. I thought I'd never see you and Chrissie again," she said, moving into his welcoming arms.

"We were wondering about that. No one knew where

you were or even if you'd survived the hurricane."

After giving her a light, friendly hug and a kiss on her cheek, he moved back to observe her in detail. "I hope you're not planning on going back to Florida anytime soon."

"Not for a while."

"Mommy, you have big boo-boos. We've been worried about you. Where were you?" Chrissie asked, looking up at her mother.

Evelyn bent down to hug Chrissie. "I was safe from the worst of the hurricane, in Orlando with Aunt Lainey's friends."

"Come home with Daddy and me. We won't let you get hurt again."

"Now that's the best idea I've heard in a long time," Thomas said.

Evelyn smiled and her hazel eyes twinkled. "You're both such a welcome sight. I can't remember when I've been so happy. Where are Mom and Dad? And Lainey?"

"We're going to meet them at home," Thomas said.

"You are staying there while you're in town, I hope?"

He nodded. "I'm looking forward to it, as usual."

****

Thomas stepped out of the shower, dried off, and slipped into the white terry cloth robe that William and Katherine kept for him in the guest bedroom. He'd been the last to retire and still was not ready for bed. Thinking he would like a brandy, he padded into the kitchen.

"Thomas! Couldn't you sleep?" Evelyn asked, sipping a cup of tea.

"No. I've had a lot on my mind lately, you mostly."

Evelyn's cheeks flushed. "I'm sorry, Thomas. I couldn't call out for a while after the hurricane."

"I'm just glad you're safe now. We have all been so worried, even Brad and Julie, whom you haven't met yet."

"Brad and Julie?"

"Julie Moss and her fiancé, Brad. They've been staying with me until their home is built," Thomas said. "They're good friends of mine and they both love Chrissie. They're looking forward to meeting you."

Evelyn was still for a moment, thinking of the huge mistake she'd made. "But, I thought that you and Julie…"

"Still reading the tabloids, I see."

"I could hardly miss it. I saw the tabloid on James's coffee table," Evelyn said.

"I'm curious. Was that before you married him or after?"

"Before." Evelyn said.

"You don't suppose he placed it there intentionally, do you?"

Evelyn nodded. "Yes."

"That explains it."

She sighed.

"Well, that's all in the past. What are you going to do about James?"

"I've already filed for a marital separation. After the hearing, I'm filing for a Dissolution of Marriage. I don't know if he's received his papers yet or not, though."

"Oh boy! You want to stay out of his way," Thomas said. "Anytime you would like to come to Vegas, let me know. If there's anything at all I can do, call me, sweetie."

"Thanks, Thomas. I'm afraid I walked blindly into a fine mess."

"But you'll get out of it just fine. Just let me know when you're ready to move on. You know, we still need to have a talk. Not now, but later."

CHAPTER 13

"What is it, Evelyn? Something's wrong. Since you received the telephone call this morning, you've been so quiet," Katherine said.

"Mr. Stuart, my attorney, called. James received the separation papers late. They were delayed because of the hurricane. Oh, Mother." She sighed. "I should have listened to you. I suspect James is not only an alcoholic, but mentally ill too. He's insisting that I had an affair with Sal, that he heard and saw us together. He talks to people that aren't there. I think he might be schizophrenic."

"I'm sure you didn't have an affair. That's ridiculous, but maybe pursuing the idea is smart on James's part."

"What do you mean?"

"Maybe he's using adultery as a defense to countersue you after you file the Dissolution of Marriage, if he can."

"Florida permits both no fault divorces as well as fault divorces," Evelyn said. "Wouldn't you think James would prefer a no fault divorce?"

"I don't know. As an adulterer, you certainly wouldn't be awarded partial custody of Bobby, and I doubt you would be awarded alimony either."

"Mr. Stuart told me he believes James may agree to

the divorce, but that he may countersue me if I ask for even partial custody of Bobby."

"Then don't. Just get the divorce. He's dangerous, Evelyn."

"There's no doubt about that. I think he is a bit off. His temper was off-scale when he attacked me. He nearly killed me."

"You looked like a madman had attacked you when you arrived." Katherine said.

Evelyn was quiet a moment, thinking of Thomas. She still loved him. There would never be anyone else like him. Her feelings for him still filled a large space of her heart. She shouldn't have married James. Initially, she'd been overwhelmed by her attraction to him. After she'd gotten to know him better and learned to despise his addiction to alcohol, she'd been repulsed.

There'd never been the deep love she'd felt for Thomas. But she'd given as much as she could to James while they'd been together.

"If you give up the custody suit and don't ask for alimony, it's my guess that you will have your divorce in no time at all."

"More than likely. I'm not interested in alimony anyway, Mother. I don't want one penny of his money and not one share of his investments or his company. I don't care about that, but I do want Bobby safe."

"Bobby's fifteen-years-old. In three years, he will be eighteen. He can visit you anytime he wants then. If James is mentally ill and Bobby needs a guardian, the court will appoint one."

"But who would they appoint?"

"If there is not a grandparent or close relative, then perhaps one of James's partners. That would be better than sparking James's wrath."

"I'll have to think about it."

"I wouldn't take too long."

"I'm just thinking about Bobby's welfare, Mother. He shouldn't be around James at all. If James continues on his current path, more than likely, he will cripple Bobby mentally and physically," Evelyn said, her deep concern evident in her voice.

Katherine rubbed her forehead and said, "You may be right. But, dear, if you will excuse me, I'm getting a headache and I believe I'll take an aspirin. This all brings back memories of the horror of my first marriage, memories I've tried to bury. I'd rather not resurrect them."

"I'm sorry if I've upset you, Mom. If you feel a little better after you take the aspirin, I'd love to go to that new store you told me about." She shouldn't have burdened her mother with her problems. Of course she didn't want to think about her past and what she'd gone through.

"I'd love that. There is a new Italian restaurant that just opened up in Scottsdale. Let's have lunch there," Katherine said.

Loaded down with packages, the two women returned hours later. Laughter trilled through the house. Home early, William greeted them at the door and helped them in with their purchases.

"Dad! You're home early," Evelyn said, pleased to see him.

He nodded. "Put your goodies away and I'll bring out cold lemonade for all of us while you're doing that. If I know my wife and daughter as well as I think I do, I'm sure your feet are tired."

"You're right, Dad, but I won't be long," Evelyn said, hurrying off to her room.

"And neither will I," Katherine said.

Gathered in the spacious family room in front of a wide plate glass window that overlooked the city, William said, "I wanted to talk with both of you about a disturbing phone call I received from one of James's partners today. The call was from Vince."

Tendrils of ice slithered up Evelyn's spine to the base of her neck. Her hair felt like it was standing on end. "Is there something wrong?"

William sighed. "James was arrested in Tucson. He was there on business in regards to the hotel he and his partners are building."

Evelyn nodded. "What happened?"

"James was staying at a five-star resort, just as he usually does. Around ten p.m., he bolted into the lobby barefooted, wearing his undershorts. Blood was dripping down his bare arms and chest. His legs were cut and bloody. Drunk and hysterical, he insisted a maniac had broken into his hotel room and had killed his wife and children. He escaped through a small bathroom window he'd knocked out," William said, running his long fingers through his hair. "The police checked with the hotel's registration desk. James was the only one that had checked in. They called James's partners to check on you, Chrissie, and Bobby. Chrissie is with Thomas, Bobby is away at boarding school and you are here with us in Scottsdale. They arrested James. He resisted. They restrained him and Baker-Acted him into the Saguaro Clinic in Tucson."

"So, he's not far away."

"Not far at all. His partners flew into Tucson, agreeing their longtime friend and partner must go through treatment for his alcoholism. Without exception, they insisted James have a psychological examination. James agreed to stay at the facility and undergo therapy for six weeks. He has been diagnosed as schizophrenic/bipolar and is an alcoholic on top of it. He needs intensive treatment. After six weeks, James will be free to leave. The doctors have told Vince that when he does leave, he will more than likely need to be on medication for perhaps the rest of his life."

"You were right," Katherine said to her daughter. "He is mentally ill."

"You realize that if James does not stay on his medication, he will be a danger to society and most of all to you, Evelyn," William said.

Evelyn's face paled. She nodded and said quietly, "I know."

"Do you understand what a schizoaffective disorder is?" William asked.

"I've heard of it, but no one I've ever known has ever suffered from it until now," Evelyn said.

"First of all, it's a difficult and rare disorder to accurately diagnose. The term is used when the patient is neither schizophrenic nor manic depressive. It's odd because some of the patients may have symptoms of both schizophrenia with or without mood symptoms. From what I've been told, James does have mood symptoms. This type of disorder often includes delusions and hallucinations well after the patient's mood has stabilized."

"Sounds dangerous…just like James. He sees and hears a character named Steve. He says he was a friend of his mother's, too," Evelyn said, drawing her brows together. "Now I understand why he insisted he was seeing and talking with Steve."

"Steve is as real in James's mind as you are," William said.

"Then he believes I had an affair not only with Sal, his partner, but with the dry cleaning man, too. I'll bet that's what Sal wanted to tell me when I was first dating James," Evelyn said.

"I expect it is. Too bad you never had an opportunity to find out before you married him."

"I'll bet James interrupted your conversations every time he saw you with Sal," Katherine said.

"That's exactly what happened."

"You may be able to file for an annulment rather than a divorce in that case," Katherine said.

"Unfortunately, maybe not. Most mentally disturbed people do not really believe that anything is wrong with them. That's one of the reasons they don't stay on their meds," William said.

"I don't suppose anyone would actually want to believe that there is anything wrong with them," Katherine said.

"What else did the doctor say?"

"James exhibits paranoia and bizarre behavior," William said.

"There's no doubt about that."

"The diagnosis is better than if he had been diagnosed with schizophrenia, but not as good as if he'd only been diagnosed just with a mood disorder," William said.

"What kind of medication will he need to take?" Evelyn asked.

"You'll need to speak with the doctor about that, but he has been in at least six dual diagnosis rehabs since he was nineteen years old. His partners covered his illness up because not only were they all childhood friends, but

James had become the primary financial backer of the company."

"Then he probably inherited his money after his father died," Evelyn said.

"More than likely," Katherine said, shaking her head. "If you'd only known, you could have saved yourself months of agony."

Evelyn nodded. "But I was so drawn to him; I thought I was in love with him. There were a few moments of happiness, but then he turned into a monster. He was like Dr. Jekyll and Mr. Hyde."

"That's exactly what a patient with his diagnosis would be like. Medication will help him, but only if he stays on it," William said.

"Maybe in time he will be all right."

"Don't get your hopes up. I almost forgot to tell you, Dr. Staddler asked me to tell you to call him as soon as possible."

"Thank you, Dad. I will."

"His phone number is written down on a pad in the kitchen."

Evelyn rose and moved toward the kitchen. Before she could pick up the telephone to place her call, it rang.

"Dr. William O'Malley's residence. Evelyn McMann speaking."

"Mrs. McMann, this is Dr. Staddler. I'm the psychiatrist who has been treating your husband at the Saguaro Clinic in Tucson. I spoke with your father this afternoon."

"Yes. Dad told me you had called and has informed me of my husband's diagnosis. We have been discussing this. Dad explained the terminology and prognosis. James is to undergo six weeks of treatment and therapy, isn't he?"

"Yes, he has agreed to do that," Dr. Staddler said.

"Thank heavens. He will be all right if he stays on his medication then, won't he?"

"Oh no, Mrs. McMann. That is especially why we are calling. James needs much more than six weeks of therapy and treatment. That is only what he has agreed to. James is seriously mentally ill. I have recommended a program of one to three years of intensive treatment along with daily medication. Your husband refused. If he doesn't take his medication when he leaves the facility, he will be a virtual time-bomb. *You* are his first target. He sees you as a threat to his livelihood and to his son. This imaginary character named Steve constantly reinforces his belief," Dr. Staddler said. "He is very dangerous, my dear."

"Can't you hold him there? Force him into treatment?" Evelyn asked, desperately hoping they could not only for his sake, but for hers too.

"No. By law, I'm afraid the most anyone can do now, unless he hurts himself or someone else, is to Baker-Act him into a treatment center for observation for a three-day period."

"Then that means there must be thousands of unmedicated, mentally ill people mingling in society," Evelyn said, her voice betraying her horror.

She could hear the doctor's heavy sigh over the telephone. "I'm afraid so, Mrs. McMann. Most are mingling in society, homeless, and in jails. Few are where they should be…on medication or in a treatment center. With proper treatment and medication, James could be an asset to society."

"Someone needs to convince him of that," Evelyn said.

"We've tried. His partners will continue to try, but you must not. If you will pardon my intrusion, my advice to you is to stay far away from your husband until he has long-term treatment and is on medication."

"Thank you for the warning, doctor. I appreciate it."

"You're welcome. Take care, Mrs. McMann."

"I will."

"Goodbye then."

Shaken, Evelyn moved back into the living room. Sitting down, she faced both her mother and father. "Dr. Staddler tells me James is seriously mentally disturbed, that he has refused long-term treatment. He will be violent and dangerous once he is released if he doesn't stay on his medication."

"That's right," William said.

"Then I should fly back to Florida, do whatever I may need to do with the attorneys, pack up, and fly back to Arizona."

"You can't stay in Lainey's villa. It's in serious need of renovation. The fence was torn down by the hurricane, the balcony upstairs was ripped off, and it needs a new roof. More than half of the shingles are gone and a blue tarp covers half of it," Katherine said.

"I wouldn't need to stay there, although it is still livable."

"You wouldn't be comfortable. You're not thinking of going to James's home, are you?" Katherine asked.

"Yes. That's where my writing materials and clothing are. I need to pick them up."

"Evelyn dear, you don't know if the home is even still there. The hurricane may have demolished it."

"I'll call Sal or Vin and find out."

"For heaven's sake," Katherine said. "You've barely

recovered from your injuries."

"I'm all right. I'll call Brenda, the nurse I met at the hospital. Maybe I can stay with her," Evelyn said.

"Have you spoken with her since the hurricane?" Katherine asked.

"I'm sure she's all right. I haven't heard from her. She was going to stay at her brother's home in Melbourne, which she considered safe. I'd think if anything had happened, she would have called."

"Not if she was injured. Melbourne was hit hard. Maybe you should call her," Katherine suggested.

"Maybe so. I'll call her work now. She should be at Indian River Memorial," Evelyn said, moving back into the kitchen.

"I don't think Evie should be going down to Florida," William said.

"Neither do I. Someone could pack up her things and send them to her," Katherine said.

"That would be best. I'll suggest it."

Evelyn returned to the living room. She was pale and appeared stunned.

"Is something wrong, Evelyn?" Katherine asked.

"Both she and her brother were injured in the hurricane. She was at work, but is still recovering from minor injuries. They are both living with friends now. If she'd stayed in her home in Sebastian, she might not be alive. Several trees from the wooded lot next door crashed into her home. The roof is gone, windows broken, and most of the home was destroyed. She doesn't have much left and will need to find temporary shelter or continue staying with friends until her home is rebuilt. Her brother's home is in similar condition. I don't know how either of them survived," Evelyn said.

"Thank God she wasn't killed," Katherine said.

"They were both lucky. Evidently, it was a mess in Indian River and Brevard County. There was a shortage of gas, long lines of people just waiting for ice water, and lots of looting going on," Evelyn said. "If Greg hadn't been there, I would have been with Brenda."

"You won't fly in now, will you?" Katherine asked.

"I'll wait a week, but I won't fly into Orlando. Rental cars are scarce, hotels too. I may want to stay at Lainey's, damaged or not, but Brenda did give me the number of her friend's home. She said to be sure and call."

"Well, at least you have a contact. Where will you fly into?" Katherine asked.

"Palm Beach or Ft. Lauderdale. I'll be fine. I need to go soon while James is still in Tucson. I'd like to go no later than next week. I'll make the reservations and call Greg Stuart. I believe I'll drop the custody suit for Bobby. I'm sure Vince and Danielle will see that Bobby's well taken care of."

"That's one of the smartest decisions you've made this year, especially since schizophrenia has genetic tendencies."

CHAPTER 14

James paced back and forth across the new patio facing the beach. The home had withstood the brunt of the hurricane force winds fairly well. The eye had struck above Boca, in Ft. Pierce. What had been damaged had been repaired immediately except for some of the landscaping. It would take time for that to grow back. Even so, he was glad to be home. No one would ever force him to go into another rehab or mental facility. Nor would they force him to take the damned medication they had given him. It made him feel strange, but worse than that, he'd gained weight like he always did when they put him on meds. He looked like a fat man now.

He'd always hated fat people. He had no respect for them. He thought they were gluttons, that they didn't have any self-control. But now, he'd learned that a simple thing like medication could cause one to become overweight. He had no one but himself to blame. He knew that. The police had Baker-Acted him, but he had agreed to stay at the Saguaro mental facility for six weeks. He'd hated it and hadn't been able to stay that long. They couldn't make him. Not when he was there of his own free will. Damn doctors there were crazy. He'd left last night.

Caught a plane into Palm Beach and taken a limo home.

The doctors at the clinic had tried to convince him the voices he heard weren't real, nor was Steve. That was pure bull shit. Steve had been with him since he was a kid. When he was nineteen, he'd saved him, broken his fall when he'd taken a tumble off the roof a couple of years ago. He could have been killed. Steve was real and he knew it.

As far as Evelyn's infidelity went, he'd seen her in a hot clinch with Sal more than once, just like he'd seen the dry cleaning man undressing her in their bedroom. How could they tell him he hadn't seen those things, that they weren't real? He'd seen his first wife with lovers, too, many of them. Steve had told him to be on the lookout, that she was unfaithful and that the child she carried wasn't his.

He opened the top of the bottle of Haldol, moved to the wastebasket, and emptied it. Then he emptied the bottle of Lithium. No more. He'd go back to his support groups, ease up on the drink, and he'd be as good as new.

"Hell, you're good as new now, man," Steve said. *"Have a gin and tonic. You'll feel better than ever."*

Maybe Steve was right. He poured himself a gin and tonic. One for Steve, too. Steve never drank, but he thought he might at least have a welcome home drink. He left it for him awhile. Steve didn't touch it, so James drank it. By mid-afternoon, he was feeling just like his usual self.

Late that afternoon, Steve urged him to see Evelyn. A danger to his livelihood and to his son, he needed to take care of the situation. Pronto! If he didn't, Steve said she'd take everything he had, even his son. That frightened James. Somewhere, deep in his heart, he still cared for her. He didn't believe Steve.

He knew Evelyn didn't think he knew where she was. But he did. He'd had a detective on her. He knew everything from the time she'd left him up to now. She thought he didn't know her sister's address on Orchid Island where he was fairly certain she would be staying, or that she'd flown back to Florida yesterday from Phoenix, but he did. She'd flown into Palm Beach. He laughed. Wouldn't it have been funny if he'd met her when she'd departed the plane? He would have loved to have seen the expression on her face.

James took a shower, shaved, and dressed in his khakis and a Hawaiian shirt. Slipping on his brown loafers sans socks, he grabbed the keys to the Cadillac and left. About halfway up U.S. 95, he heard Steve talking to him.

"Steve! I was so absorbed in my own thoughts, I didn't notice you get in the car with me."

"Yeah. Thought you would like a little company and something good to drink for the drive. I brought you this too. Thought you might need it."

James glanced down on the empty seat beside him. A pair of surgical gloves, a 12-inch knife, masking tape, rope, a blanket, and a flask full of whiskey. What the hell? He didn't need any of those things, except maybe the masking tape to make Evelyn shut up while he explained things to her.

He drew his brows together. Where had Steve gone? He turned around and looked in the back seat. Not there. He shook his head and took a gulp of whiskey. Big raindrops spattered on the windshield. Thunder rumbled. A mile up, the rain began falling in sheets. A tropical rainstorm, common in the summertime to the sub-tropical state of Florida, obstructed his vision. Lightning struck.

Thunder exploded. The Cadillac veered to the right, near the shoulder, almost too near.

James squinted. He could barely see through the rain. Maybe he should stop for coffee.

"No, man. Keep going," Steve said.

By the time James arrived Ft. Pierce, he knew what he was going to do to Evelyn.

Steve was smart. Now he knew what the surgical gloves and knife were for, along with the other stuff. He'd never need to worry about Evelyn again. He hoped Chrissie was with Thomas. He didn't want to do the same to her.

"A man's gotta do what he's gotta do," Steve said.

CHAPTER 15

Lost in a spiral of confusion, Evelyn pushed her hair back from her face. It was raining outside, coming down in sheets. Thunder exploded and lightning zigzagged across the darkened indigo sky.

She rose from the sofa she'd been sitting on that faced what was left of the garden. They'd been lucky. The hurricane had all but taken out the high rise condos across the street.

Balconies had been ripped off, windows smashed. It appeared that something had sheered the entire face of the building off. It was being re-built now, but much of the area appeared to be a disaster zone.

She hadn't liked the telephone calls she'd received, both at noon and again this evening. Hang-ups. They could have been wrong numbers, but she didn't think so. She had a bad feeling that something was drastically wrong, that her life was in danger. She didn't need to stretch her imagination too far to guess where the source of the danger lay. She'd just flown home yesterday. James was still hospitalized. Or was he? Had he left? Walked out of the facility? Wouldn't someone have called her?

Most of the time, she relied upon her instincts. She

hadn't when she'd married James.

She knew her mother had been right when she'd pleaded with her to wait before she accepted his proposal, but in the end, she'd ignored her mother's warning and her own niggling suspicions. The chemistry she and James had shared had overpowered her own good sense.

Thank God for Thomas. At least she didn't need to worry about Chrissie. But, if something happened to her, if she were murdered, Chrissie would only have one parent. Chills snaked up her spine and spread to every bone in her body. She rose and ran up the stairs to her bedroom. She tossed her cosmetics, a change of lingerie, capris and a tee to match into a tote bag and dashed back down the stairway. With her keys in hand, she left through the connecting garage.

She started the car, clicked on the garage door opener, and backed out. She drove north on Ocean Drive. When she stopped at the light at Beachland Blvd., a white Cadillac turned left, toward the small development of townhouses she'd just left. A man had been driving the car, but the rain was coming down so heavy that she couldn't see him clearly.

James maybe. If so, he'd walked out of the facility. She didn't want to see him, not now, especially not now. Not ever, if she could help it, except maybe in the courtroom. When the light turned green, she followed Ocean Drive until it connected to A1A and drove toward the turn off to Sebastian.

On her way, she called her new friend Brenda on her cell phone. Evelyn felt as though she'd known her for years. She'd been married to an alcoholic too and she had no love for James, not after having seen Evelyn's injuries.

"Brenda. I'm so glad I was able to reach you. I'm in

Florida for a few days and I'm staying at Lainey's. I'm on my way up to Melbourne now and would love to see you. Would you like to meet me somewhere?"

"Evelyn, it's good to hear from you, but what's wrong? You sound upset. Where are you now? You sound like you're on your cell phone. It's beginning to cut out."

"I'm just at Wabasso Road, the turn off to Sebastian on A1A."

"Come on over. Turn left at the light and come up Highway 1. It's shorter to my friend's house than driving up A1A. They're out of town and I don't have any plans tonight. Why don't you stay here? We can catch up."

Evelyn grinned. She could hear the excitement and the pleasure in Brenda's voice. "Sounds like a good idea. Maybe I'm crazy, but for the last hour or so, I have had a strong feeling that my life is in danger. I thought I saw James turn toward the townhouse when I was leaving Vero."

"You did right to leave. Don't you have a restraining order on him?"

"No. I didn't have time when I filled the Dissolution of Marriage."

"Restraining orders aren't always effective. Sometimes, they just make someone like James crazy," Brenda said.

He's already crazy.

"Did you bring any clothes?"

"Just my cosmetics, a change of clothes, a sweater…forgot the pajamas and robe."

"You can wear a pair of mine. Plan on staying a couple of days," Brenda said.

"Are you sure? I don't want to impose."

"Don't be silly. It will be fun. Just go up highway 1,

turn left on highway 192 until you reach Barnes and Noble. It will be on the left side of the street. I'll meet you there and you can follow me. I don't live far from there."

"Okay. Thanks. See you in a while."

She felt so much better. If James had planned to harm her in any way, it wouldn't happen tonight.

CHAPTER 16

With a wide grin on his face, James parked in her driveway, blocking Evelyn's escape. She would have only one other avenue, back door, facing Ocean Drive. He snickered. No problem. Steve was waiting for her there. He got out of the car and pulled the hood of his black windbreaker up. He wouldn't bother ringing the bell. That would be stupid. She'd never let him in.

James took a credit card from his wallet and laughed while he did it. Bobby had showed him this trick. If the front door was locked, and it might not be, he'd just trip the lock with the card. It would be a quiet, easy access, and he'd catch her unaware.

With the credit card in hand, he slipped the masking tape into the pocket of his black raincoat. Boldly, he slid the credit card into the lock. The door opened easily. The condo was quiet, too quiet. The TV wasn't on, neither was the CD player. Had he missed her? Was this the right condo, or had the detective made a mistake? He went room by room through the house, knife in hand. He checked the closets and saw her clothing. Anger seethed through him. He grabbed the rod and yanked it down. It was the right condo, but she wasn't here.

He felt his face redden. He trembled. Running down the stairway, taking two at a time, he left.

Slamming the front door, he turned, slashed an X in the center of it, and jammed the knife into it. The next time he'd follow her, make sure she was home. He'd catch her in bed asleep. This time, the knife he carried wouldn't be driven into the door. It would be driven into her heart.

"Better this way, man. Better to catch her later, when she's asleep, just like you said. She'll think she's having a nightmare, last one she'll ever have."

James laughed hysterically and headed back out through the driving rain, back to Boca.

He squinted, trying to see through the rain. "Steve, look in the glove box. Take out my glasses. I need them to see through this mess."

Where did Steve go? He'd just heard him. He shrugged his shoulders. He wasn't there. Damn. He had to have his glasses. Blurred taillights appeared in front of him, a motorcycle maybe. He braked to slow down, reached over to take his glasses from the glove compartment, swerved, slid, and lost control of the car. As it slid off onto the soggy shoulder, it flipped, and rolled down an embankment. The sound of metal grinding against metal, glass breaking, and a shrill scream invaded his ears. Something rammed into his chest. He felt a sharp pain, then an odd feeling of being separated from his body. Darkness enveloped him, along with a deadly silence. He barely heard the sound of the rain beating on the car.

Without warning, he was standing outside in the rain looking at a mangled white Cadillac that had evidently gone off the embankment above. The driver must have been blinded by the heavy rain. Odd, it was pouring, but he couldn't feel the rain. Why hadn't a tow truck come? When had the accident happened? Evidently, the police hadn't come either. The car looked like a mangled version of the car he owned. He walked around to the back of the car. At the angle it was at, he could see a twisted license plate. He walked closer to read it. It was his. He felt sick. Was he dead? He looked around. It seemed to him he was very much alive. A white light appeared and beckoned him. He walked toward it. At the end, three figures waited. Funny, they reminded him of his mother, Clarissa, and Elaine. Behind him were at least a dozen other women. One looked like the stripper he'd seen at the Oasis Gentleman's Club in Phoenix. They waved to him and then disappeared along with the white light. They were the last people he wanted to see. Why had they been there? To lead him to hell?

Suddenly, he was back in his car. He was in such pain. Someone was trying to pull him from the car.

****

No one had seen the accident. Once the weather had cleared, the highway patrol noticed his car and began their investigation. They presumed the driver was dead, but no body was found.

CHAPTER 17

Evelyn spent two days at Brenda's. They rented a boat for a day and had a wonderful time. Her spirits were lifted and she no longer felt danger threatened her in any way except maybe for a gator or two sliding off the river bank. She felt a huge sense of relief, as though a heavy burden had been lifted.

"Thank you for everything, Brenda. I feel fine and I'm sure everything's okay now."

"I don't know, Evelyn. Even though you feel as though everything's all right, it might not be. I'd really like to follow you home. At least there will be two of us if anything is wrong. Anyway, if everything's all right, I'd like to go to some of the little shops along Ocean Drive today."

Evelyn brightened. "Okay. That sounds perfect. We can have lunch, too. The Ocean Grill's open."

"I'm glad that wasn't destroyed," Brenda said.

"Being right on the Atlantic, it was a miracle that it wasn't."

"Especially since so much of the beach was lost. Just a second. I'm on the night shift today. I need to take my uniform with me."

"You can change at Lainey's townhouse."

Brenda turned and displayed her gorgeous smile. "If everything is okay."

By the time Evelyn reached Orchid Island, she was beginning to feel she might not have been right to assume everything was okay. She was glad Brenda was behind her. Turning into the townhouse area, she parked in the driveway just in case. She wasn't comfortable enough to pull into the garage.

Brenda parked in front of the house and stopped midway to the door. "Don't come any closer, Evelyn. Call the police. Now."

"Why? What's wrong?"

"Just call. Tell them it's an emergency."

Evelyn didn't question Brenda. She ran back to the car, grabbed her cell phone, and called 911. A squad car was there within minutes.

"Mrs. McMann? Evelyn McMann?" the officer asked Brenda.

"No. I'm Brenda Wagner, her friend. This is Evelyn McMann."

"We just got home and there's a knife in my front door, a big slash, and an X carved into it."

"You didn't go in, did you?" the officer asked.

"Not yet."

"I'm glad you called the police instead of taking a chance and going in on your own. Even with your friend with you, it could have been dangerous. Wait here. I'm going to take a look around," the officer said, moving to the door. "Did you leave the house unlocked?"

"No, I wouldn't do that."

"Well, it is now. I'll go in and look around. If it's safe, you can come in with me, see if anything is missing, but from the looks of this door and the knife, I'd say the intruder was after you."

Nausea rose in Evelyn's throat. "I wonder if it was James?"

"James?"

"My husband. I'm going through a divorce."

"You were right to leave when you did," Brenda said.

While the officer was inside searching, the sheriff's car pulled up. "What's the problem here?"

Evelyn repeated what she'd told the police officer.

"Well, this might be the work of your estranged husband, but I'd say it's safe to say he won't be bothering you again."

"Why? What's happened?" Evelyn asked.

"Neither your parents, your sister, nor your former husband, Thomas Valentino, could reach you by telephone. You need to turn your cell phone on or charge it."

She nodded.

"I was sent out here for two reasons. First of all, to make certain you were all right and had not been harmed in any way. I'm happy to see you're fine and have fortunately been away for a few days. Secondly, Mrs. McMann, we believe your estranged husband, James McMann, was killed in an automobile accident traveling south on US 95 between Vero Beach and Ft. Pierce," the sheriff said.

"You believe?"

"The car was registered in his name, but his body wasn't found."

"When did this happen?" Evelyn asked.

"Saturday night."

Evelyn glanced at Brenda. "I left for my friend's home

about an hour before that. I just missed him, if it was him."

"I imagine it was him. You were lucky," Brenda said.

"I understand you filed charges of abuse and a Dissolution of Marriage," the sheriff said.

Evelyn nodded.

"I looked into the abuse charges when we couldn't locate you. He just about beat you to a pulp, didn't he?"

"He did a good job of it," Brenda said. "I was her nurse in the hospital."

"We'll check the prints on the knife, if there are any, but I'd bet they are those of James McMann. Now, if you will excuse me, I'll just check with the officer and make certain everything is all right inside and around the house."

"I can't believe what a narrow escape you had," Brenda said.

"Luck, or my angels were with me."

"I'll say."

When the sheriff and officer emerged from the house, they removed the knife from the door and slipped it into a baggy. Moving toward her, the sheriff said, "Looks safe inside. I could tell someone had been in there, unless you yanked down the rod in the closet yourself and left it there with the clothing on the floor."

Evelyn chuckled. "No, sheriff. Even when I'm in a hurry, I'm not that messy."

"Well, we'll be going now. You might want to give your attorney a call, as well as Mr. Valentino, your parents, and Mr. McMann's partners."

"Thank you, sheriff. You too, officer."

"Call us anytime, anytime at all, if there's a problem."

"With all of those calls, I don't think you will have

time for shopping," Brenda said with a tone of disappointment in her voice.

"Excuse me a moment, Brenda. I don't feel so well," Evelyn said, running for the bathroom.

Feeling as queasy as she did, there was no way she could go shopping or to lunch. Just like yesterday and the day before for the past few weeks, she was sick to her stomach. After she had lost everything she'd eaten, she washed her face and brushed her teeth. Must be some kind of virus she'd caught. She glanced in the mirror over the sink, smoothed her hair, and returned to Brenda.

"What's wrong?"

"I haven't been feeling so well for the past few weeks."

"Sick to your stomach a lot?"

Evelyn nodded. "Nerves, maybe."

"Has this just been in the mornings? Or all day?"

"Mostly, in the mornings."

Brenda raised her eyebrows. "I hate to ask you this, but is there any chance you might be pregnant?"

Evelyn blanched.

"Judging by your expression, I would say there is."

"I was using birth control, but there were two or three times before that...well, we didn't exactly plan to..."

"It only takes one time without using precautions."

Evelyn groaned.

"Have a couple of Saltines, make your calls, then let's go to the pharmacy and pick up a pregnancy test," Brenda said.

"I can hardly bear the thought that I might be pregnant with James's child, but I'd better find out," Evelyn said.

"You have calls to make. I'll go to the store and pick

up the kit," Brenda said.

"You're an angel."

The calls to her mother, Lainey, and Thomas didn't take long. No one was home, nor did anyone answer their cell phones. She'd left messages to everyone that she was at Lainey's now, safe and sound. She also left messages that James had evidently been killed in an accident Saturday night.

Greg Stuart, who had proven to be of invaluable assistance, didn't hide his relief. Evelyn wouldn't need to worry about James harming either her daughter or herself. He realized James had been mentally ill and had suffered from the terrible disease of alcoholism. With the exception of the tremendous amount of money James McMann had amassed, he hadn't lived a happy life. Without treatment for his disease or his chemical imbalance, his life would remain the much the same. For those reasons, Greg considered his death a blessing to all, especially himself. Still, if his body wasn't found soon, he would insist Evelyn follow through with the Dissolution of Marriage. So far, they had only dropped the custody suit.

By the time she'd made her calls, Brenda had returned.

"Positive?"

Evelyn nodded. "I don't want to have his child. I should have been more careful."

"I know of a wonderful doctor."

Evelyn sighed. "I've never believed in abortion, unless one was raped."

"Are you Catholic?"

"I'm a convert."

"Perhaps this might be the time to reassess your thinking."

"Maybe so. It's not just me I have to think about. It's Chrissie, too."

"Do you want to think about it over lunch? Soup and crackers might be good for you about now."

"Let's do that."

Though the decision was one of the most important of her life, it didn't take long for Evelyn to make up her mind. Besides the custody battles she would have with James, the baby might very well have a mental disorder and possess a tendency toward alcoholism.

Ordering a piece of apple pie al a mode, Evelyn said, "I've made up my mind. I want to see the doctor just as soon as I can get an appointment."

"Wise decision. I'll call now. He may be able to fit you in."

Evelyn waited while Brenda called. She couldn't keep her hands still. Taking her straw from the iced tea glass, she twisted it around and tied it.

Brenda hung up and grinned. "Nervous?"

"Yes. I want this done as soon as possible."

"How about later this afternoon?"

"You're kidding. How did you arrange that?"

"My secret. You know I am in the medical field. I know a lot of doctors," Brenda said with a wink.

CHAPTER 18

The police had searched the area where the accident had occurred thoroughly for the body, but without success. The case remained in limbo. Knowing that JVS development must resume business and that the incident must be finalized, especially for Evelyn to move on personally, Vince and Sal pressed for the case to be closed, but James could not be declared legally dead until either his remains were found or seven years had passed after he had been reported as missing.

This complicated everyone's lives. Bobby needed a guardian, accounts needed to be settled, and bills paid. Vince and Sal decided the best thing to do would be to read James's will and go on from there. The automobile he had been driving had been so mangled that no one actually believed that James had lived through it or could have possibly escaped the wreckage. Because he was missing and they believed he had died, they agreed that all of his close relatives must be notified.

Under the Florida Homestead Act, if James died while they were married, the marital home on A1A would automatically go to Evelyn, along with the Mercedes and the yacht. After James's abuse and in light of the fact that she had filed a divorce, she had no desire to live in the home on A1A. Since it had been Bobby's childhood home, she wanted him to have it.

The bank accounts and stocks and bonds were held in a trust that would eventually go to Bobby. Since James had granted Vince a Durable Power of Attorney to act in his behalf if he were rendered unable to handle his affairs, Vince had the power to pay all bills, deposit checks, and buy and sell stock or other assets for James. He would see that everything would go on just as before. Bobby could continue in military school just as he had been. Both he and Sal, as well as James's half-brother, Kyle, were beneficiaries of million dollar life insurance policies that were held in irrevocable trusts and would remain so for seven years or until James's body was found.

Evelyn was interested only in Bobby's welfare. He would be fine. Vince would make sure of that. What had shocked her the most was the discovery that James had a half-brother. He'd never mentioned him. It was too bad they hadn't been closer. Just having an aunt and an uncle would have added so much to Bobby's life.

Thinking that more than likely they would never see James alive again, Vince and Sal decided that in celebration of his life, they would all fly to Bimini in the Bahamas and stay at the cottage he had reserved for them before.

Evelyn vowed to remember James at his best. He had not been himself under the influence of alcohol. He hadn't been able to control the disease without a support group, nor had he been able to correct his chemical imbalance without treatment. She knew that she would never be with him again and vowed to find out all she could about mental illness. Had James inherited the chemical imbalance? How had it occurred? And when? Would his son follow his path? She hoped not. James's partners said he'd been fine until his late teens.

After Vince read the will, Evelyn returned to the beach house that afternoon and began packing the things she wanted to take with her to Arizona. While she was away, the home was to be repaired from the hurricane's damage. For now, the house held memories of unhappiness and terror. It was Bobby's childhood home, the only home he'd ever known, and he pleaded with her to come back soon, at least for Easter. She'd agreed she and Chrissie would be back unless Bobby changed his mind and wanted to come out west instead.

After she'd packed her things, Bobby pulled out old family albums with pictures of him as a baby and pictures of his mother and James. He had James's azure eyes, but he had the thick hair his mother did, along with her fine lips. Bobby was trim like Elaine, and often he wore the same happy smile she did.

"I hardly remember my mother. I was only three years old when she was killed," Bobby said with tears in his eyes.

"But you know she loved you very much. I can see that by the pictures," Evelyn said.

Why had some of the photos been torn in half? Someone had been torn out of the pictures. She'd caught a glimpse of a skirt in one. Had James hated her so much he had torn her image away?

Bobby sighed. "I don't think Dad liked me very much. He was always working or with his partners. It seemed like I was in the way. I hope I don't have to stay at school on holidays anymore."

"You can always visit Chrissie and me. Has anyone

talked to you about where you will be living?" Evelyn asked.

"Yes. I like Vince and Danielle, but I'd rather live with you," Bobby said.

"But we'll see each other a lot. Your Uncle Kyle will be here soon. How long has it been since you saw him?"

"I guess I saw him when I was little, but I don't remember him."

"Well, it will be interesting to see your aunt and uncle. I'm looking forward to meeting them."

"All the other kids I know have aunts and uncles, brothers and sisters. I hope I like Uncle Kyle and Aunt Jennie, and I hope Uncle Kyle likes sports."

"He's due to arrive tonight. You won't need to wait long to find out." Evelyn had no more finished her sentence when the doorbell rang.

"Someone's here. I'll get it," Bobby said to Terry, who was already on his way to the front door.

"Mr. McMann called earlier and said he would be coming in early," Terry said, moving into the living room.

Evelyn started. Her hand flew to her heart.

"I meant to say, Mr. and Mrs. Kyle McMann," Terry said with a half-smile. "I'm sorry I startled you."

"You needn't apologize," Evelyn said.

At the sound of a man's deep voice, Evelyn moved toward the entry hall.

"Evelyn," Bobby said. "This is my Uncle Kyle and my Aunt Jennie. Uncle Kyle, Aunt Jennie, this is my friend and stepmother, Evelyn McMann."

Evelyn took one look at Kyle's clear blue-green eyes and Jennie's chestnut brown eyes that reflected her sincerity. She knew she liked them immediately. Kyle, taller than James had been, had curly, sandy hair, heavily sun-streaked. His physique was that of a runner. *He doesn't resemble James at all. He must take after his mother.*

Kyle smiled and shook her hand. "I'm sorry we have to meet like this."

Jennie smiled and said, "It's been so long since we've seen Bobby. It's wonderful to see him again and a pleasure to meet you, Evelyn."

"And you."

"You're staying with us, aren't you Uncle Kyle, Aunt Jennie?"

"Please do," Evelyn said. "There's plenty of room."

"All right then. We'd love to, providing you will allow me to take you to dinner," Kyle said.

Evelyn grinned. "We would enjoy that, wouldn't we, Bobby?"

He nodded. "Yeah. That would be great."

"Come in, sit down. We'll see that your things are placed in the guest room. Would you like some iced tea, lemonade?" Evelyn asked.

"Iced tea, please. Thank God you didn't offer us an alcoholic beverage. Neither of us drink," Jennie said.

"At most, I may drink one glass of wine at dinner, though quite often, not even that," Evelyn said. "My parents didn't drink alcohol except for celebrations and even then, only a glass or two of wine."

"I can't imagine how you ever ended up with my brother," Kyle said, shaking his head. "James was brilliant. He had a good heart, but the alcohol took him down. Of course, you know that. Poor guy. You probably know we were half-brothers. His mother was a drinker. Our father taught us from an early age not to touch liquor, but sadly, James did. Well, after our parents' divorce, his mother raised him, so he didn't have all of the benefits I did. Both his mother and he attended a support group. But, oftentimes, it's just not enough."

"No. It isn't."

"Where are you from?" Jennie asked, changing the subject.

"Scottsdale, Arizona. My father's a psychiatrist there. I'm going back in a few days, after the memorial service," Evelyn said.

"That's a long way from here," Kyle said.

"It is, but I'll be back for Easter with my daughter if the renovations on the house have been completed."

"Where is your daughter now?" Jennie asked.

"In Las Vegas, Nevada with her father."

"How old is she?" Jennie asked.

"Four and a half."

"Her dad's a famous singer," Bobby piped up.

"Oh?" Jennie said. "Tell me more."

"His name is Thomas Valentino, Aunt Jennie."

"Oh, my God! He's more than famous. I've always wanted to see him in person," Jennie said.

Evelyn laughed. "We're good friends. When you visit Las Vegas, let me know. I'll send a couple of complimentary tickets to his show."

"I'll hold you to that," Jennie said. "My friends will be so envious."

"Uncle Kyle, do you like sports?"

"Sure do. In fact, would you like to take a run on the beach with me? I'm stiff from the airplane ride," Kyle said.

"Yeah!"

While Kyle and Bobby were out, Jennie approached the subject of Bobby. "He seems like a good kid."

"He is, but he is starved for attention. James paid little attention to him," Evelyn said. "There's something else I'd like to talk with you about, Jennie. I'm glad the guys are out running,"

"What is it?" Jennie asked, moving closer to Evelyn.

"Did you know that James was recently Baker-Acted into a mental facility in Tucson?"

"No, I didn't, and I think Kyle would have mentioned it if he'd known. What was his diagnosis?"

"Schizoaffective. He is also an alcoholic."

"I've never heard the term schizoaffective. What does that mean?"

"It's a bipolar disorder coupled with schizophrenia."

"Oh, my lord," Jennie said, her face blanching. "Kyle and I have always believed that as well as being an alcoholic, James's mother was not quite right in the head."

"It can be an inherited illness."

"Has Bobby shown any symptoms?"

"Not as far as I know. But I believe with treatment and medication, mentally ill people can live normal lives. I'm a freelance writer, Jennie. After being with James and being exposed to the nightmare of living with an un-medicated person, I promised myself to do extensive research on the subject. I've found a national group I intend to join. It's NAMI, the National Association for Mental Illness. Through it, I can educate myself and others."

"That's a noble cause," Jennie said. "If Bobby shows signs of being bipolar or schizophrenic, becomes mentally ill, do you think that Vince and Danielle will be able to cope?"

"More than most people could. Vince is also Bobby's godfather and knew James for many years."

"I've been concerned about Bobby for a long time just knowing James was an alcoholic. I didn't know he was mentally ill," Jennie said.

"Neither did I. Bobby said he hadn't seen either of you since he was a baby, since his mother was alive."

"But it wasn't because we didn't want to see Bobby. For one, Kyle couldn't handle seeing James deteriorating in front of him. Secondly, after Kyle was divorced from his first wife, Clarissa, she moved to Boca Raton."

"Was that after James's first wife was killed?" Evelyn asked.

"I think so. But, in any case, Kyle discovered James had an affair with her before she was killed in the boating accident," Jennie said.

"Boating accident? What happened?"

"It was odd. Kyle told me that Clarissa was an excellent swimmer, she didn't drink, and she'd been on many boats. Of course, James wouldn't mention it to you."

"No. He never mentioned Kyle either. Nor did he mention that he was an alcoholic. He had many secrets."

"How long did you know him before you married him?"

"I'm ashamed to admit, only a few months. James was in a rush to marry," Evelyn said.

"I expect he was. He didn't want you to discover his secrets."

"More than likely, you're right. You mentioned a boating accident."

"It made the headlines. Someone I know saw it and sent the clipping to us. James and Clarissa had been boating in the Bahamas. Evidently, she fell off the boat and into the motor," Jennie said.

"Oh, my God! What a terrible death."

"Ghastly. We never heard from James after that. We wanted to see Bobby, but not James."

"I understand," Evelyn said. "Do you have children?"

"No. We've wanted to, but haven't."

Just as well, Vince and Danielle will be Bobby's guardians.

"We have a collie…that's our baby. And I manage a little boutique in Beaufort. That keeps me busy. I love it. In fact, I would like to own one of my own."

"You might just get your wish in a few years, Jennie," Evelyn said, thinking of the million dollar insurance policy James had left to Kyle.

"I doubt it. Unless I find someone who would be a wonderful partner, we just couldn't afford it."

Evidently, Vince had kept the insurance policies quiet. That was probably wise, since James had not been declared legally dead.

"I feel badly about James's accident and his mental illness. We should have kept in touch with him. Perhaps we could have helped him."

Evelyn took a deep breath. Though she'd always tried her best not to judge others, she couldn't stop her thoughts. *You should have kept in touch. James was alone in the world with the terrible, debilitating disease of alcohol…and with a chemical imbalance too.* He needed to know he was loved, that he had a family somewhere. More than likely, he was afraid his partners and wives would find someone else and leave him.

I don't think he had a positive self-image. How could he have? That was no excuse for his abuse and attempt on her life, but she could forgive him. He was sick and probably wasn't aware of what he was doing. The sober James, the one on medication, would never have done it.

But the other one…the one crazy with intoxication…had he murdered the other women?

"You couldn't have cured his disease or changed the fact that he had a chemical imbalance, but perhaps just knowing he was loved would have helped."

"Yes, you're right. But we will keep James in our prayers. Perhaps he survived the accident and is lost and stunned."

"Maybe," Evelyn said. "But they said the automobile was totaled. I don't think he could have survived."

"Probably not. But while Kyle and I are here, he can tell Bobby about the good times he and James shared as children. There must have been a few."

"That would be nice," Evelyn said. "Would you like a tour of the house?" she asked, changing the subject. "You would probably like to freshen up. I'll show you where your room is. There's a large bath and powder room just off the guest suite. I'll ask Mae to help you unpack and iron anything you would like."

"Thank you. That's quite a luxury for me."

While Evelyn was giving Jennie a tour of the elegant home, the doorbell rang. She left Jennie in the guest suite and went to greet her unexpected callers. "Vivian! I didn't expect you."

She laughed. "It's not only me. We should have called first. Sam, Vince, Danielle, and Sal are behind me. I knew James's brother and his wife were coming in today. We thought you might need food, so we have brought dinner for all of us. To tell you the truth, we want to see Kyle and his wife. Vince and Sal met him years ago, at Mrs. McMann's funeral…James's mother's funeral."

"How did she die?"

"In a fire. James was gone. It came as quite a shock to him. They believe she fell asleep and left a cigarette burning, but no one really knew," Vivian said.

"How old was James?" Evelyn asked.

"I'm not sure. He was away at the University of

Florida at Gainesville when it happened."

"I thought he had a degree from Harvard," Evelyn said, puzzled.

"James didn't tell you the truth about himself, did he? He went to the University for two years. After that, he went to work for Vince and Sal as a salesman. When his father died, he inherited quite a sum of money from him and invested the bulk of it into the business," Vivian said.

"My God! Will I ever know the truth about the man I married?"

"Does it really matter now?" Vivian asked.

"I guess not. By the way, just so I know who to expect, who did Sal bring today?"

"No one, dear. Watch out. He's had his eye on you for a while."

Uh-oh. I wonder if James knew that?

"I wasn't aware of that," Evelyn said.

"You mean you never noticed?"

"No." *But I'll bet James did.*

CHAPTER 19

They could not hold a memorial service for James since no one knew if he was alive or dead. Instead, Evelyn asked that four masses be said for him. As far as the family went, they decided to hold a very informal memorial service on the beach in Bimini near the bungalow they had rented.

Vince, who had known him for most of his life, told about their early experiences together, the courage and determination James exhibited in creating and helping their business become the success it was. Bobby followed, saying some particularly kind things about his father. He talked about how James had taught him to fish, tie his shoestrings, take care of him when he'd been sick, in general, all of the things his dad had to do while he was growing up without a mother.

Kyle surprised her by taking the podium and speaking about what a super little brother he'd been while they were young boys. She knew she should say a few kind words about James since she was the widow. Even though now she was an estranged spouse, she buried all thoughts of his abuse and told of his big heart and generosity. Everything that had been said, and that she said of James, was true. It was simply his illness, chemical imbalance, and non-acceptance of either that had caused his life to go awry. With that, she silently forgave him for anything he had ever done or said to her or to Chrissie.

Afterwards, Vince, Danielle, Sal, Kyle, Jennie, and Bobby walked down the beach to the village and James's favorite coffee shop, chatting about all of the good times they'd shared with James. Later, they went fishing, just as James would have done. If he'd been there, he would have said it was a perfect day.

The following day, they were silent, engrossed within their own thoughts on the return trip to Boca. When everyone had left except Vince, Danielle, Kyle, Jennie, and herself, Bobby said, "Do me a favor, please. If I ever get sick like Dad did, make sure I go to a treatment center and take my medication even if I don't want to. I don't care if you tie me up and pour it down my throat."

Evelyn laughed. "First of all, I hope you're never sick like your dad was, but if you are, you have my promise."

"And mine," Vince said.

"Ditto," Danielle said.

"You got it, kiddo," Kyle said.

The next morning, Bobby left for the Admiral Farragut Academy. Later, Jennie and Kyle departed for Beaufort, S.C., leaving only herself to go through James's personal belongings. She thought of James and the evening he had picked her up wearing his black jeans and blue plaid shirt. He had looked so handsome, but what she didn't know was that just below the surface lurked mental illness and an addiction to alcohol.

Evelyn opened his closet and hesitated. What if James had somehow survived the accident? What if he came back? She decided to wait. If he hadn't been declared dead by Easter, she would do it then.

A knock came at the door.

"Come in."

"We wondered where you were. You don't need to sort out James's clothing," Mae said. "Terry and I can do that for you."

"Thank you. I've decided it might be too early to do that. I'm thinking we should wait …just in case."

"We can do that," Mae replied.

"You have your own things to pack and a plane to catch for Arizona. We'll take care of anything that needs to be done from here on," Danielle said.

"What about his desk?" Evelyn asked.

"I'll take care of his office," Vince said.

"No. I mean his desk in the office here."

"I'll take care of it," Vince said.

"Are you sure?"

"Yes. It will be no problem."

"Just promise, whenever you're here, we will get together," Danielle said.

Evelyn smiled. "That's a promise."

"Before you leave, sit down a moment, Evelyn. I have a surprise for you," Vince said. He moved to the closet, opened it, and took a file box from the top shelf. "James wasn't himself for a long time before he died." He opened the file box, searched for a moment, then pulled out a long, narrow blue velvet box. "I was with James when he purchased this. It was to be your anniversary gift this year. It's yours, and we want you to have it. You deserve it for loving him and putting up with him for as long as you did while he was in his sorry state. Besides, you have been a wonderful friend."

Evelyn took the blue velvet box and opened it. Inside

was the most stunning emerald and diamond necklace she'd ever seen. She smiled and glanced up at Vince and Danielle, her eyes full of water. "Thank you. I know he loved me."

Vince nodded. "It was his illness, Evelyn. He wasn't himself."

"If he'd taken his medication and continued going to his support group, I do believe your marriage would have worked. At heart, James was a wonderful man when he was sober and in his right mind," Danielle said.

"He was brilliant," Vince said, "even with his grandiose ideas."

CHAPTER 20

Evelyn wore a peaceful smile on her face the following day when she leaned back in the airline's first class seat and closed her eyes, more than ready to depart on the six-hour trip to Phoenix.

She was looking forward to writing every morning again, first thing after she'd had coffee and watched the news. James had despised the time she had spent writing. It was as though he'd been jealous of it. She realized that was the beginning of the end of their relationship. His dislike and treatment of Chrissie had killed any love she had ever felt for him. It was over with. She could go on with her life and close the chapter of her marriage to James McMann.

With the steady hum of the plane, she fell asleep. When she awoke, they were landing. She took out her mirror, brushed powder over her cheeks and blush. After she'd applied lipstick, she ran a pick through her hair, fluffing it up. She knew her mom and dad would be there to greet her.

Lainey, wearing a dour expression on her face, greeted her once she was in the baggage claim. Her clothing was rumpled. Her eyes were red with circles under them. Her mother and father were nowhere to be seen. Lainey eyes brightened when she saw her.

"You're a welcome sight, kiddo. I'm so glad you're home."

"So am I. But where's Mom and Dad? What's wrong?"

"I tried to call you this morning, but you were already gone. That, or your cell phone was off. Unfortunately, I have bad news. Let's sit down a moment and I'll tell you."

"What's going on? What's happened? Mom and Dad aren't here. Neither are Thomas and Chrissie."

Lainey sat and motioned for Evelyn to do the same. "It's Dad. He had a stroke last night. Mom's still at the hospital."

"Oh, jeez. Is he all right?"

"We don't know yet. He's in intensive care. Both Mom and I have been up all night waiting to hear. Let's go pick up your bags and get something to eat. I haven't had a thing since dinner last night. That seems like centuries ago. I left Sedona early this morning after Mom called. You must be starved."

"I am, but at least I've had peanuts. What happened to Thomas and Chrissie?"

"They'll be in soon. In fact, by the time we have something to eat, their plane should be arriving. Thomas asked me to book a room for him."

"He didn't need to do that," Evelyn said.

"But Mom is so upset. She really doesn't have room. Not with you, Chrissie, and me too."

Evelyn smiled. "We could stay at the villa. It hasn't sold yet."

"I don't think that's a good idea. After all, there's a chance James is still alive. And if he is staying there, in one of the models, it could be dangerous."

"I believe that's pretty far-fetched, but I think Thomas would agree," Evelyn said.

"The restaurant's to the right just ahead."

Evelyn nodded and followed Lainey. She hadn't known her dad had been ill and wondered what had brought the stroke on. She was anxious to hear more.

"I told Thomas that if we weren't at the gate to meet us here," Lainey said.

"Good. He and Chrissie are probably hungry."

"A table for four, please. The other two will be in a little later. We'd like the quietest spot you have," Lainey said.

The waitress nodded and led them to a table in the far corner.

"Thank you. When Mr. Valentino comes in, he'll be asking for the O'Malleys. Please show him and his daughter to our table."

"Of course." the waitress said, leaving menus.

"Maybe we should wait for Thomas and Chrissie," Evelyn said.

"No. I don't think they will be in for another twenty or thirty minutes. Anyway, they would rather we have something to eat. They know how impossible I am when I'm hungry."

Evelyn laughed. She'd forgotten just how irritable Lainey could be when she was hungry.

After they'd placed their order, she said, "Now, I'd like to hear about Dad's stroke, what led up to it, and how serious it was. Did he need surgery?"

"Mom said Dad had had high blood pressure for quite a while. He suffered from a hemorrhagic stroke."

"What's that? I didn't know there were different kinds of strokes."

"Well, neither did I. But there are. Dad's was evidently caused by a cerebral hemorrhage."

"Did he require surgery?"

"No. The only time surgery is needed is if a lot of bleeding occurs or if the patient's condition is deteriorating. Dad's wasn't."

"Is he paralyzed?"

She nodded. "His left arm is."

"What will he do if he needs to retire? He's always been so active."

She nodded. "Dad's a type A personality and has high blood pressure. We can only pray he recovers."

"Dad is strong willed. I imagine his recovery will be speedy, especially if there's a good after treatment program."

"There is."

"Did the doctor discuss it with you or Mom?"

Lainey nodded. "His blood pressure needs to be regulated, the pressure inside his brain needs to be lowered, and he needs to be monitored. We need to make sure the head of his bed is in a partially upright position. Mom, or whoever takes care of him, needs to watch for restlessness, confusion, headaches, and problems with commands."

"What do you mean by problems with commands?"

"For instance, if we ask him to hand us the paper and he doesn't understand, then we will know there's a problem," Lainey explained.

"So you're saying his brain may not connect right away."

She nodded. "He'll need to avoid straining, excessive coughing, and lifting. We'll need to monitor his temperature. While he's bed, he will need to wear special stockings to help prevent blood clots."

"Dad's not going to like this," Evelyn said, shaking her head.

"No, he won't. But, if he recovers, these details might keep him alive."

"What if—"

"We don't talk about the what ifs, should haves, or would haves in this family, remember?"

"But…"

"Okay. Just this one time."

"Our parents are getting older."

"Not that old."

"Anything can happen at any time," Evelyn said.

"That's always been true."

"If Dad should become disabled, will they move into a retirement home?"

"Never. Mom and Dad have talked about this."

"Oh! What then? Move into a luxury townhouse, hire a nurse or two to live-in, plus a good-looking chauffer for the limo?"

Lainey laughed "You've got it."

"What if Dad passes before Mom?"

"I've thought about that. If that happens, we need to see that Mom opens the dress shop or boutique that she's talked about."

"I think she should do that anyway. Thanks for filling me in," Evelyn said.

"Even though some of the details of Dad's stroke were rather technical, I felt as though it was necessary that you understand everything."

Evelyn nodded. "It just might save his life."

"Mommy!"

Evelyn turned and was smothered by Chrissie's wet

kisses. She hugged her and said, "I've missed you, dear. Did you know your Aunt Lainey was going to be here too?"

Chrissie nodded, unwrapped her arms from her Evelyn's neck, and ran to Lainey.

Evelyn rose to greet him. He kissed her lightly on her cheek and said, "Our flight arrived early. I'm glad to see you safe and sound, Evelyn. It was all I could do not to catch the first plane out to Florida to retrieve you. But, I knew my presence would have only added to your difficulties."

"Actually, I would have enjoyed your company. Danielle and Jennie would have been thrilled. I had my hands full with his brother, sister-in-law, and Bobby. It was such a strange time for everyone, not knowing if James was actually dead or stunned and roaming around the Everglades," Evelyn said.

"Very disquieting," Thomas said. "How is Bobby faring?"

"He's doing very well. James's partner Vince and his wife Danielle are his guardians. I expect that and they will be wonderful to Bobby. The biggest surprise of all occurred when James's half-brother Kyle and his wife Jennie showed up at the mansion. He's an officer in the Marines, stationed just outside of Beaufort, South Carolina, at Parris Island. James had never said a word about having a brother."

"How odd."

"I thought so at first until I heard the story. Evidently, James had an affair with Kyle's first wife, Clarissa. After her divorce from Kyle, she moved to Boca and dated James. Unfortunately, she was killed, fell into the motor of a boat while she was fishing with James."

"Was she a drinker?"

"No. She was an excellent swimmer and had been on many boats."

"It could have been an accident, or…"

"Or maybe she was pushed," Evelyn said, finishing his sentence.

"She might have been if James had been drinking."

"Or if he was hearing voices."

"My God!" Thomas said. "You were in more danger than any of us could have guessed."

"Mommy, is Bobby going to live with us?"

"No, dear."

"Why not?"

"He will be with Vince and Danielle when he is not in military school."

"Can he visit us?" Chrissie asked, placing her hands together as though she were praying.

"Of course, dear."

"Sit down, Chrissie. Let's order. We should probably be going to the hospital soon," Thomas said. "I'm glad you two didn't wait for us."

"You should have waited for me, Mommy."

"I'm sorry, dear," Evelyn said, taking a bite of her salad.

"Actually, I insisted upon ordering before you arrived," Lainey said. "I was famished and no one needs to be around me when I'm hungry."

Thomas laughed. "I remember that. Chrissie, you must forgive your aunt and mommy for ordering early. They meant well, and it was in our best interest."

"Okay, Daddy."

Lainey turned, caught the waitress's eye, and motioned her over. "They need to order now. We have a family member critically ill and we need to go to the hospital soon."

"Do you know what you would like?" the waitress asked, smiling at Thomas.

"A chicken enchilada, please, with a side of guacamole and iced tea," Thomas said. "Chrissie, what would you like?"

"Mmm. A tuna sandwich and a glass of milk."

"Make that on whole wheat for her, please," Evelyn said.

"Are we going to see Pa-pa after we have lunch?" Chrissie asked as the waitress wrote their orders down.

"Yes. Thanks for reminding me, Chrissie," Lainey said. "Could you bring the check with their orders, please?"

"Yes, miss. I'll be glad to. The order will take about fifteen minutes. Is that too long?"

"That will be fine," Lainey replied.

"Mommie, could you take me to the restroom, please?"

Evelyn rose, took Chrissie's hand and excused themselves. By the time they returned, he Chrissie's milk was waiting for her.

"I should probably call the hotel and tell them I'll be arriving after six. I don't believe my secretary did that," Thomas said.

"Oh, Thomas. You don't need to stay at a hotel. Please, stay with Chrissie and me in the villa. Lainey didn't think it was such a good idea for me to stay there, but there's plenty of room."

"The villa?" Thomas drew his brows together. "I agree with Lainey. James's body was never found. What if he is still alive? It might be much better if we stayed in a two-bedroom suite in a nice resort hotel."

Remembering she had found the French doors of her home that led from the terrace into the master bedroom suite open twice while Kyle and Jennie had been there, Evelyn nodded and said, "I think you're right." She had asked everyone who had been at their home about it, and no one had opened the doors, including Mae and Terry.

"You should clear out the villa. I'll help you," Thomas said. "Please don't even think of going there alone."

"Thank you, Thomas."

"When are they bringing our food, Daddy?"

"Soon, I hope," he said glancing to his watch.

Five minutes later, the waitress brought their food.

"You did plan to ride with us to the hospital, didn't you, Thomas?" Lainey asked.

"Actually, I reserved a rental car."

"That's something you won't need. I still have my Jaguar. If we're staying together, you won't need to rent a car," Evelyn said.

Thomas placed his hand over Evelyn's and said, "I'll take you up on that, pretty face."

Lainey glanced at her watch. "Ready, kiddos? We need to be on our way. We still have baggage claim to deal with. I've brought the SUV, so there's plenty of room."

CHAPTER 21

William sat up in his hospital bed, a wide, crooked smile on his face. He wasn't able to move his left arm, but other than that and his slow speech, he'd survived the stroke without too much damage.

"I'm so glad to find you awake, Dad. How are you feeling?" Evelyn asked.

"Like a man who's just come back from the dead. I couldn't be greeted by a more welcome sight. Here you are, you and Thomas together. I've waited a long time to see this."

Thomas glanced at Evelyn with a wide grin.

"Er...I just arrived from Florida. Lainey was at the airport to greet me. Thomas and Chrissie met us there, and here we are. I'm so happy to see everyone, you too, Thomas."

Thomas placed his arm around Evelyn's shoulder and said, "I'm happy to see both of you. For a while, I was as worried about Evelyn as I have been about you recently, Dad."

"I don't believe you need to worry about either one of us anymore...at least not for a while. I have things to do yet here before I experience my transition into the spiritual life. Being as ill as I have been, though, has given me a different outlook on life. From what the doctor said, I'll need to take it slower, maybe even retire from practice. But, that might be a pleasure, give me more time to do the things I've always wanted to, like take up a hobby, maybe do some volunteer work."

"What kind of hobby are you thinking of, Dad? I don't think I remember you mentioning anything before now," Evelyn said.

"I've always wanted to do some photography, for one. I'd also like to travel more to places I haven't been to yet."

"Sounds like you might be about ready to enjoy the gypsy life."

"I think so. I believe I would enjoy it immensely. I'm sorry I gave all of you such a fright."

"I'm just glad you're up now, and talking so well too. Mom said you had suffered a little paralysis from your stroke."

"I'm a little slow, I know. And of course, I'm sure my pronunciation of words is not as clear as usual since the left side of my mouth is kinda crooked. I can't do much with my left arm either, but it could have been so much worse. I thank God I have another chance at this life."

"Me too, Dad. You mean so much to all of us."

"Thomas, you did say Chrissie's here too, didn't you?"

"Yes. I wasn't sure if you were up to seeing her and the nurse would allow only two of us in at once."

"I'm glad you and Evie came in together. Of course I'm up to seeing Chrissie...always, until I take my last breath. Seeing my family, including you, Thomas, brings me joy. It's better than any medicine the doctor could prescribe," William said.

"That you did," Thomas said. (huh?)

"You'll be all right now, Evelyn. Everything's behind you now. It's time to start over, put all of that mess with James behind you," William said.

"I'm sorry for that, Dad. I feel my situation might have placed extra strain on you."

"Well, of course it did, but we were all worried about you. Don't think for a moment that you were the cause of my illness. Basically, it had been coming for a long time. I'd had some warnings, but ignored them. It was really the lifestyle I was living—working too hard, not taking enough time to smell the roses, so to speak."

There was a knock at the door.

"I'll get it," Thomas said, moving toward the door.

"Time's up," the nurse said. "I'm sorry, but it's Mr. O'Malley's first day for visitors. If he's feeling well enough tonight, he can see his family."

"What about my granddaughter, nurse? I want to see her too," William said.

She glanced at her watch. "Well, your time's not quite up yet. If Mrs. O'Malley would like to bring her in for just a minute after the Valentinos leave, that would be all right with me."

Thomas grinned and turned to Evie. "Well, pretty face, looks like our time's up. Sorry, Dad," he said, walking back to the bed. "We'll be back to see you tomorrow."

"You're staying at the house, aren't you, Thomas?"

He shook his head. "No. Evelyn, Chrissie, and I are staying in a suite at the hotel."

William grinned and his blue eyes sparkled. "Make the most of it, man," he said quietly to Thomas.

"I intend to."

Evelyn moved to William's side, bent, and kissed him on the forehead. "I love you, Dad. Don't let Chrissie tire you out."

"Oh, she won't. The nurse will make sure of that."

"I certainly will," the nurse said. "Now, you two may come back tomorrow, if you like."

"We will," Thomas said, and escorted Evelyn out.

By the time they checked into the hotel, they were exhausted. Thomas carried Chrissie in, sound asleep. Lying her on one of the queen-sized beds in Evelyn's room, he slipped her shoes off and tucked her in, pulling the light blanket up to her chin.

Evelyn stood in the doorway with a smile on her face, feeling as though everything was as it should be with her little family. In her heart, she knew that this right. The only thing that stood in their way was the possibility that she was still married to James. Greg had strongly suggested she follow through with the divorce.

Thomas turned and moved toward her. Meeting her in the doorway, he drew her into his arms. Her senses began to spin as she moved into him, her arms encircling his waist. Warmth flooded through her as their energies combined, growing in strength. "It's good to have you back, Evie."

She sighed. "It's wonderful to be back." *Where I belong.* "I should have come back earlier. What if Dad had…"

"But he didn't. He's going to be all right."

"I hope so," Evelyn said.

"He needs to slow down, though."

"That's hard for Dad to do."

"That's probably why he had a stroke," Thomas said.

"His spirits are up. That's a good sign. If this hadn't happened, more than likely, he would never have slowed down. He's a hard worker and a stubborn man."

"Stubborn like his daughter?"

She laughed. "Maybe."

"Being stubborn about the right things is okay. It's getting late and we need to be up early. Would you have a nightcap with me before we turn in?" They have provided us with a refrigerator and I do believe I would like a Black Russian. And you?

"I'd love to have one."

Thomas turned and moved into the living room of the suite. Following him in, she sat on the sofa. Watching Thomas prepare their drinks was a pleasure. Thomas as not only a handsome man, but he moved with grace as well. Seeing him again filled her with warmth.

"To you, Evelyn, and to your continued safety."

"Thank you, Thomas. There have been some times recently when I don't think I'd have made it without a guardian angel or two watching over me."

"I was more than concerned about you. What are your plans?"

"Well, it's difficult to say, but I think the best thing to do is follow through with the divorce."

"Do James's partners believe he was killed?"

"I think so. Vince has the Power of Attorney to act in James's behalf. He read his revocable living trust and is familiar with James's assets and liability. He didn't close any of James's accounts. In fact, although we went to the Bahamas for a very informal sort of memorial service, Vince is treating his absence as though James was on an extended vacation."

"He's playing it safe."

"It seems like it."

Thomas drew his brows together. "But it's almost as

though Vince believes he is still alive. Did you see his last bank statement?"

"The last transaction was the day he drove up to Vero Beach."

"It's feasible that he could still be alive. He may be injured, have amnesia, or just be stunned, wandering around somewhere, maybe even working an odd job."

Evelyn drew her brows together. "Is that what Greg believes too."

"Isn't he the attorney Lainey recommended?"

"Yes. He has strongly suggested I continue with the divorce in the event that James did survive."

"That's prudent. There's no point in taking risks."

"I'll need to fly back down to Florida for the final hearing."

"Then I will go with you. I won't go into the courtroom for the hearing, but I'll be nearby, just in case you need me. I don't want you going down there alone again, especially since we don't really know if James is gone."

"I would like that, Thomas. I don't think I could stay in Lainey's townhouse alone again."

Thomas shook his head. "No. I don't want you to, nor do I want to stay in the house you shared with James. I have a friend who has a vacation home on John Island. When you know the exact date of the hearing, I'll give him a call and let him know we'll be in town."

"That might be an imposition."

"He owes me a favor," Thomas said. "And he's stayed at my home in Vegas."

"Do I know him?"

"Not yet. I co-starred in his last film with him. In fact, he's one of your favorite actors," Thomas said with a wide grin.

"You're not talking about Robert…" Evelyn asked.

"Yes."

"Oh my God!"

Thomas laughed. "Now you sound just like one of my fans. Now that we've settled that, think about coming to Vegas."

Evelyn could think of nothing else she'd rather do. She certainly didn't want to live in Florida, nor did she want to live with her parents, not when Thomas was in Las Vegas and Chrissie was there a good portion of the time. The decision was easy.

"I'll need a place to live."

Thomas nodded. "I have a friend in Vegas who is on tour and would like to lease his condo. It's well furnished and has security. Would you like to see it?"

Evelyn grinned. "Yes, I'd love to. Chrissie would be so happy to have her parents in the same city."

"I think we can do a little better than that later," Thomas said with a smile.

"We'll see. One step at a time. For now, let's focus on Dad."

****

William recovered quickly, his spirits boosted by his family surrounding him. Each time he saw Thomas and Evelyn together, he knew one of his wishes would soon come true. He could have died, but he wouldn't let go of the fragile thread of life until they were truly together again. Until then, he intended to do just as the doctor ordered.

CHAPTER 22

During the short time they spent in Phoenix, Thomas insisted Evie have professional movers pack her things and Chrissie's. Except for supervising the movers, he didn't want Evelyn or Chrissie near the condo. Once the movers completed their task and placed the items in storage, Evelyn listed the townhouse for sale and drove to Vegas with Chrissie, meeting Thomas at his home.

He wore a wide smile the evening they arrived. His chocolate brown eyes twinkled. Hugging them both, he said, "At last, I have my two favorite girls living in the same town as I do. Did you have a nice trip?"

"Yes, wonderful. Chrissie was a doll," Evelyn said with a fond glance at her daughter.

"I slept almost all the way, Daddy. Are we staying here tonight?"

"Yes. You may stay as long as you like, but I will show you and your Mommy the condo that is available tomorrow morning. My friend needs to know if you will be taking it or if he should place it up for lease."

Evelyn smiled and said, "I'm sure it will be fine, Thomas."

But the next morning when she saw it, she nearly

gagged when she saw the color of the carpet. She'd never liked olive green. The furnishings were okay, but compared to the villa in Scottsdale she'd just vacated and the beach house in Florida, the place was distasteful, even to Chrissie.

"Are we going to live here, Mommy?" Chrissie asked, looking up with a hesitant expression on her face.

"It's not far from my house."

"It's close to the shopping center and movies," Evelyn said.

"I want to see my room," Chrissie said.

"And the pool," Thomas said.

Evelyn bit her lip. She didn't like it. It gave her the creeps, but if she didn't take it, they would need to stay with Thomas; not a good idea when she was going through a divorce.

"The condo has excellent security even if it is an unattached villa," Thomas said.

"That's important."

"What do you think? Even though I know you hate olive green, he's offering us a big discount," Thomas said.

"I think it's a deal," Evelyn said. She could buy a couple of throw rugs, fresh flowers, and some accessories to improve it. She wasn't buying the condo, after all. The location was good and the swimming pool was a delight.

"What do you think, pumpkin?" Thomas asked Chrissie.

She shrugged her shoulders. "I like the pool and I can come see you often, can't I, Daddy?"

"Both of you may visit me often."

"Okay, then it's a deal, like Mommy said."

"Wonderful, then you can move in right away. You still need to keep your Florida residency. We'll say you're vacationing here," Thomas said.

"That's wonderful. I'd love to have Julie and Brad over for cocktails and dinner later this week. Oh, and you too, Thomas."

"I thought maybe you had forgotten me, pretty face."

"Mommy would never forget you, Daddy," Chrissie said.

"Never."

****

While she was waiting for the final decree, Evelyn spent her days working on her novel, writing articles, and sunning by the pool. She saw Thomas frequently and longed to be in his arms once again. It was becoming more and more difficult to keep her relationship with him light. With the sale of her condo in Paradise Valley, the horror she had experienced at James's hands was quickly fading away.

That evening, she celebrated with a quiet dinner with Chrissie, Julie, Brad, and Thomas at his home. Leaving Chrissie with Thomas, she left just after midnight to drive back to the condo she had leased. The moment she opened the door, she sensed something was not as it should be. Since nothing was out of place, she attributed her uneasy feeling to her vivid imagination. After all, her work in progress was a romantic suspense. She'd written a particularly frightening scene this morning.

She drew her brows together. She'd forgotten to set the security alarm before she and Chrissie had left earlier in the evening. She turned, set it, and moved into her bedroom. Moonlight flooded into the room, highlighting a man's figure as he stood in front of the sliding glass door that led to the swimming pool.

Her hand flew to cover her heart. Hadn't she locked

the sliding glass door? If she had, she evidently hadn't set the alarm, or he'd by-passed it.

He moved toward her.

She froze. Opening her mouth to scream, her voice cracked.

He laughed, a high-pitched hysterical laugh.

Her heart pounded, her vision blurred. She screamed. Turning, she kicked her stiletto heels off and ran. The sound of his footsteps behind her quickened her pace. *Crash!* A heavy thud sounded. *Maybe he tripped and fell.*

Rounding the corner, she slid into the kitchen and grabbed the heavy marble rolling pin. Clutching it in her hand, she moved quietly in the darkness to the front door. Opening it, the alarm went off. How had he gotten in? Had he been in the house the whole time, since before she and Chrissie had left? Maybe he had come in while they were at the pool. O.M.G.! He could have been watching her while she was in the shower. Visions of the famous scene Janet Leigh had played in the film *Psycho* flashed in her mind.

"Gotcha now, bitch. You can't get away from me."

Had he seen her? She couldn't see him, didn't know where he was. She waited and hoped he couldn't hear her pounding heart. He crept by her, didn't see her. Wasting no time, she brought the heavy rolling pin down on his skull. He fell. Her mouth curved up at the corners. "Wanna bet? Watch me now."

Taking no chances, she dropped the rolling pin and ran out the door. The sprinklers came on, drenching her. Barefooted, she ran faster. Rounding the front of the Jaguar, she opened the door and slid into the driver's seat. Pressing a button, she locked all of the doors.

Wiping the perspiration from her forehead, she

started the car. She tore off into the night. Her throat was dry. She began to tremble. Had it been James? She thought the voice had been his, but it could have been her imagination. She hadn't gotten a good look at him. All she knew was that he was tall, maybe 6-foot, with dark hair and a high-pitched laugh. It could have been anyone, anyone who wished her harm.

****

Thomas awoke to the loud ringing of a telephone. "Dammit, I thought I turned the ringer off." Turning on the light on the end table next to the bed, he answered. "Hello?"

"Mr. Valentino, the security alarm is going off at Eddie Germaine's villa. We've called, but no one answers the telephone. Mr. Germaine asked that we contact you if there was a problem."

Thomas drew his brows together. *Evie should be home by now.* "Have you contacted the police?"

"They're on their way to the house now."

"Good. I have a key to the house. I'll drive on over," Thomas said.

"That won't be necessary, Mr. Valentino. There was a break-in. You would only place yourself in harm's way."

"But my ex-wife may have been in the condo when the break-in occurred."

"The police will handle the situation."

He thanked them and hung up. Running his hand through his hair, he slipped into the robe lying at the foot of his bed. Moving to the picture window, he gazed out into the raging storm. The villa wasn't far. Evelyn should be here soon. A car drove up and turned into the circular driveway. He rushed to the front door, turned off his alarm system, and opened the door.

"Evelyn! What happened? You're drenched. The alarm people called. They said there was a break-in at the villa."

Evelyn stood on the front porch under the overhang. "I hit him, knocked him out, maybe even killed him."

"What did you hit him with…your fist?"

"A rolling pin."

Thomas laughed. "The marble one."

She nodded. "Good thing I kept it."

Thomas reached out, took her hand, and drew her into the foyer. "Come in the house. You'll catch a cold out there. Where are your shoes?"

"I kicked them off when he ran after me."

"Good thing. Those were so high I don't know how you could walk in them much less run. Let's get these clothes off," he said, leading her into the bathroom. He dried her hair and began to peel her wet clothing off. "Help me, Evie. You need to take your clothes off and slip into this terry cloth robe. It's mine, so it will be too large, but it will keep you warm. I'll get us each a brandy, then we'll talk."

"Thank you," she said, her voice trembling and weak.

He hugged her, kissed her on her cheek lightly, and said, "You're going to be all right. You're here now."

She nodded. "I was okay until after it was all over."

"But you handled yourself well. You got away."

"Even if I haven't taken a self-defense class yet."

"Do that right away. You might not have a weapon at hand next time."

After he'd left the room, she took the rest of her damp clothes off and slipped into Thomas's robe. She was still shaken from the episode. Had it been James? She wasn't sure. Making her way into the family room, she fell back onto the oversized leather sofa.

When Thomas entered, he handed her a glass of brandy and said, "Do you feel like talking about it yet?"

"I don't know who it was. It could have been anyone."

"Anyone?"

"A common thief, a rapist."

"But he was waiting for you."

"I know. Maybe he saw me somewhere, like the grocery store, and followed me home. He could have come back later and entered the house while Chrissie and I were at the pool. Maybe I didn't lock the front door after I carried in the groceries," Evelyn said.

"The police will find prints," Thomas said. "Or him, if you knocked him out."

"I hope so, but if he was just stunned and got away, they may not find him."

"Why not?"

"I think he wore gloves; plastic, surgical gloves."

Thomas raised an eyebrow. "The police will want to question you."

She nodded. "I expect so. I don't want to go back there."

"I don't want you to. I think you should stay here with me," Thomas said.

"But the divorce isn't final yet."

"It will be soon."

"I hope so," she said. The phone rang again. Evelyn started, spilled her brandy on the oversized robe she wore.

"Excuse me. It's probably the police. I called them and told them you were safe and here with me," Thomas said. "They may want to speak with you."

Evelyn sighed. She rose and went into the guest bath to wash off the sticky brandy from her hands and the side of the glass. After she'd dried her hands, she came back into the room and sat back down on the sofa.

She wondered what she could tell the police that would lead to the intruder. It had been dark, she had been terrified. It could have been her soon-to-be ex-husband, she couldn't be sure. It could have been anyone tall, lean with dark hair.

"Who was on the phone?" she asked.

"The police. The intruder got away. There were no fingerprints. You were right. He wore gloves," Thomas said.

Evelyn sighed with relief. "At least I didn't kill anyone."

"You don't have the killer instinct, sweetie. You're still cold," Thomas said, drawing Evelyn into his arms.

"I know."

He bent to kiss her on the cheek. She turned, wrapping her arms around his neck. The robe fell open, exposing her luscious figure.

His lips met hers. Desire filled her as it had not since they had last been together, since before their divorce. Her fear forgotten, she melted into his arms.

"Stay with me tonight. Sleep with me," Thomas said softly.

"I could do nothing else," she said. "I need to feel safe, to be in your arms."

He picked her up and carried her into his room. Lying her gently on his bed, he slowly removed her robe. The evening was one he had waited for, but more than he had ever imagined. Their lovemaking began slowly, gently, then became urgent and demanding. By dawn, neither of them had slept more than an hour or so. It had been the sort of lovemaking one dreams of, fantasizes about.

The following day, Julie called and insisted Evelyn stay with her and Brad in their new home. She offered her guest room to Evelyn. Not wanting to leave Thomas, but realizing, if James had been the intruder, his anger would further be incited if she stayed with Thomas, she reluctantly accepted Julie's gracious offer.

"I'm sorry you're leaving, pretty face. I was hoping you would stay," Thomas said.

"It's just that..."

"You don't need to explain. I understand. I'll bring your things over to Julie's this afternoon. You don't have your decree yet, and being here with me might incite James's wrath," Thomas said. "Call Greg Stuart and find out if he has the date for the hearing yet. I'm anxious to get this over with."

The following morning, Evelyn called Greg and relayed what had happened.

"I think I can push date of the hearing up. I'll let you know by this afternoon."

The rest of the morning, Evelyn was restless. She couldn't sit down for even a minute. Moving out to the pool, she swam twenty-one laps. Sitting on the pool steps a few moments to rest, her cell phone rang. Hoping it was Greg, she hurried to answer before voicemail clicked on.

"If you can make it, we can arrange the hearing next Tuesday morning."

"I'll be there," Evelyn said, knowing she would go alone if she had to.

CHAPTER 23

Vince took a sip of his steaming hot coffee and opened the weekly Hollywood gossip rag that Danielle so often brought home.

Eddie Germaine's Villa Broken Into
Intruder Vanishes After Being Wounded by
Resident, Evelyn Valentino, Thomas
Valentino's Former Wife and Current Flame.

Vince read no further. Remembering the violent attack upon Evelyn, he picked up the cell phone and punched in the last number she had given him.

"Dr. O'Malley's residence. Katherine speaking.'

"Hello Mrs. O'Malley. I've been trying to reach Evelyn. Your number is the last she gave me for a contact. Do you know where I might reach her?"

"She asked that I not give her number out, but I'll be happy to give her your number and message so that she can return your call."

"I would appreciate that."

"I hope I haven't bothered you," Vince said.

"Of course you haven't. In fact I'll call her right

away."

"Thank you," Vince said, leaving his contact number.

A half hour later, Vince called Thomas.

"Hello? Who did you say is calling?" he asked, placing the call on the speaker phone.

"Vince, I've heard a lot about you from Evelyn."

"I'm guessing you called because you read the news about the break-in," Thomas said.

"That's right. Is Evelyn okay?"

"Yes. It was a close call and she was pretty shaken up. She stayed here last night, but our friend Julie Moss came for her this morning. We were afraid that if James were still alive, his anger would be incited if he heard Evelyn was staying at my house."

"You're right about that. James was a jealous man, more so than most."

"Have you heard any news about him?" Thomas asked.

"A wristwatch belonging to James showed up in Ft. Pierce not long ago," Vince said.

"Ft. Pierce? That's close to where James had the accident, isn't it?"

"Yes, very close, but it really tells us nothing. Someone could have found the body and removed his valuables."

"Or James could have pawned the watch himself," Thomas said.

"Kyle's home was broken into several weeks ago while he and his wife, Jennie, were on vacation," Vince said.

"Who's Kyle?" Thomas asked.

"James's half-brother. At the time of the accident, they hadn't spoken with each other for years."

"Was anything of value missing?"

"Jewelry, a coin collection, items of Kyle's clothing, and several of Kyle's childhood family albums."

Thomas groaned.

"That points to the fact that James may very well have survived the accident. I know of Julie Moss. She is famous, a wonderful dancer, but does she have an adequate security system?" Vince asked.

"The best," Thomas replied.

"That's a relief. There's something else you might be interested in knowing. James's son, Bobby, swears he saw his dad looking into his dorm window a week or so ago."

"But no one has heard from James, have they?"

"No. Nor has he withdrawn funds from his account," Vince said.

"He may have a Swiss account or maybe one in the Caymans."

"Maybe."

"If he's alive, I wonder why he doesn't come forward," Thomas said.

"Maybe he doesn't want to. He's a sick man and needs treatment."

"Poor guy. As sick as he was or is, he must not have had much of a life," Thomas said.

"Probably not. But, changing the subject, how are Evelyn and Chrissie?"

"Evelyn's doing well. She's become good friends with Julie, who is introducing her to an editor from one of the largest publishing houses in New York. Julie says her novel is wonderful," Thomas said with a proud note in his voice.

"Fantastic. I'm really proud of her. She put up with a lot with James. What about Chrissie? Danielle and I miss them both," Vince said. "So does Bobby."

"She's fine. Say! If you and Danielle don't have anything planned for New Year's Eve, I'd love for you to come as my guests for our Special. Julie, Brad, her partner, and I have worked Chrissie into our routine. She's quite a little professional. It's a surprise for Evelyn."

"We'd love to, but Bobby, Kyle, and his wife, are coming for Christmas and staying through New Year's."

"Well then, bring everyone. Plan on staying at my home. I'd love the company, and I'd like to meet Evelyn's friends."

"That's an offer I can't refuse, nor would I want to. If I did, Danielle, Bobby, Jennie, and Kyle would never forgive me."

"We'll look forward to seeing you. In the meantime, I'm sure Evelyn would love hearing from you. She has a cell phone, so you can reach her directly," Thomas said, giving Vince her number.

CHAPTER 24

Julie was in the middle of a routine with Chrissie when the doorbell rang. Instinctively, she knew who it was and why he had come. Rather than let either the maid or doorman answer, she cut the routine short.

"I'll get it," she said.

When she opened the massive front door, she saw that she'd been right. Thomas stood with a wide grin on his face.

"If I'm right, you are here to pick up Evelyn."

"You couldn't be more right, but it's always nice to see you, Julie. You're looking wonderful, a little flushed, though. Did I disturb something?"

"Nothing that can't be started up where I left off. Actually, I was just in the middle of a new routine with Chrissie. Come in. She's packed and ready. She'll be happy to see you. Would you like something to drink?"

"The usual."

"At this time of day, that would be lemonade, wouldn't it?" Julie asked.

"Yes," Thomas replied.

"Lemonade it is, but first, I'll tell Evelyn you're here."

Thomas sat on Julie's sofa. Even though the hearing

wouldn't take long, there was no way he was going to allow Evelyn to go to Florida alone. He had not been able to reach his friend Robert, so he had decided to fly down for the hearing and back that evening. It would be an exhausting day, but he felt the less time Evelyn spent in Florida, the better. It might have been different if Robert had been there, but he was filming in Spain.

"Thomas. I didn't know you were going with me."

"Hey, pretty face," he said, rising. "I've missed you. Of course I'm going with you. We're taking my plane instead of a commercial airline. You'll want to cancel your reservation."

Evelyn smiled. "Thank heavens. I wasn't looking forward to going alone, but I want it over with."

"So do I. We're coming right back after the hearing. I hope you're agreeable to that."

"Definitely. This is one time I don't want to linger in Florida. I've talked with Greg, and I am also resuming my maiden name. Soon, I will once more be Evelyn Anne O'Malley."

"Better than McMann," Thomas said.

"But not as good as Valentino," Chrissie said, running into the room.

"Where did you come from, pumpkin?" Thomas asked, glad that she had spoken up in his favor. It was exactly what he had wanted to say.

"Julie and I have been rehearsing. Mommy, why isn't your name the same as mine and Daddy's? James isn't here anymore."

Thomas gazed into Evelyn's eyes. "Maybe your mommy's name will be Valentino again soon, pumpkin," Thomas said.

"Is that true, Mommy?"

"We'll see," Evelyn said with a smile in her voice.

****

Evelyn sat on Julie's sofa beaming. Still living with Julie, her novel was nearly finished. Van, her editor, had already begun editing her work. With a movie deal on the horizon and the promise of a future with Thomas, she couldn't have been happier.

Tomorrow, Christmas Eve, her parents and Thomas's parents and grandmother would arrive. Julie and Brad expected their loved ones to arrive from New Orleans. With all of the company, it promised to be a grand celebration that neither family had had for years, if ever.

Though Evelyn would join Thomas and her parents at his home for Christmas Eve, they would join Brad and Julie for a celebration on Christmas Day.

On Christmas Day, Thomas wore a wide grin as he placed his arm around Evelyn's shoulder. "We have a special announcement to make. On Valentine's Day, we will renew our wedding vows, er…be married again in Virginia City, Nevada. We would like all of you to join us. William smiled, tears of joy streaming down his cheeks while Chrissie broke loose of his firm grip and ran to hug her mother and father.

"You're marrying Daddy again? Can I be a bridesmaid?"

"Yes, pumpkin. You may be a bridesmaid."

"Is Julie going to be the maid of honor?"

"No, darling, but I am going to be a bridesmaid," Julie said.

"Then who will be the maid of honor?"

"Your Aunt Lainey," Evelyn said.

"What about the best man? Will that be Uncle Dan, Daddy?"

Thomas smiled and nodded.

"Why did you decide upon Virginia City? Mom and I would have loved for you and Evelyn to be married at our home in Paradise Valley," William said.

"Well, we wanted to be married after my show in Lake Tahoe. Besides that, both of us wanted to see Virginia City. Evelyn is researching it for another novel," Thomas said.

"It's a fascinating historical town. We also thought if we were married in St. Mary's Church, our marriage would survive anything."

"Isn't that the church that was burned down in the fire of 1875?"

"Yes. It was re-built by Father Mieneke."

"It's an unusual church," Katherine said. "You know how much I love Victorian architecture. St. Mary's Church is considered one of the finest examples of Western Victorian architecture."

"You've seen it?" Evelyn asked.

"Yes. Your father and I spent a little time in Virginia City years ago."

William smiled and placed his arm around Katherine's shoulders. "On our third wedding anniversary."

****

Everyone who had been invited for Christmas stayed through the week. By the time New Year's Eve arrived, they were all looking forward to seeing Thomas and Julie's Special.

Vince, Danielle, Kyle, Jennie, and Bobby arrived, excited to see Evelyn and to meet Thomas. Julie mesmerized Vince, Kyle, and Bobby with her beauty and charm while Brad delighted Jennie and Danielle, who had actually swooned over Thomas.

Bobby was ecstatic to see Evelyn and Chrissie. He refused to leave their sides and swore that once he graduated, he would attend the University of Nevada in Las Vegas just so he could visit them often. That touched Evelyn's heart, yet she feared if James was still alive, it might draw him near.

Thomas and Julie's New Year's Eve Special thrilled everyone. Their performance and voices had never been better. Yet it was Julie and Chrissie's routine that drew the biggest applause of all. "Somewhere Over the Rainbow" and their encore, "On the Good Ship Lollipop," once performed by Shirley Temple, brought rave reviews. Chrissie was following in the star's steps, on her way to a tremendous career in show business.

Following Chrissie and Julie's performance, Thomas dedicated a heart-rending love song he had written himself to Evelyn. After the song, he concluded with an announcement of their engagement.

Chapter 25

James had kept track of Evelyn, hoping that she would obtain happiness with Thomas after he had ruined her life and that of Chrissie's with his alcoholism and his illness.

Sitting in the back of the room, he wore a slight smile when Thomas announced their plans to wed again in Virginia City. Sad things had worked out as they had, he rose to leave the room.

He was glad that he had come to Las Vegas to speak for his support group at their annual conference. If he hadn't, he would never have known of Thomas and Evelyn's plans. That was one wedding he wasn't going to miss.

He'd arrived in Vegas the day after Eddie Germaine's home had been broken into and wished that they'd caught the culprit. He was fairly certain that if they hadn't, it would be him that they blamed. He was well and sober now. He wished Evelyn and Chrissie only happiness.

CHAPTER 26

When they returned to Thomas's home for a late night breakfast, a large bouquet of yellow roses awaited with a card attached to the ribbon that was tied around the vase that simply said, *"Congratulations! Wishing you much happiness."*

CHAPTER 27

Vince, Danielle, and Bobby arrived in Virginia City, sunburned from skiing Heavenly Valley. Sal arrived later, just in time for the wedding, with a new blonde on his arm. Following were Julie and Brad, who had just arrived from a show in Reno.

William, grinning from ear to ear, arrived with Katherine, Lainey, and the handsome shaman from Sedona. It had been his fondest desire to see Evelyn and Thomas joined in matrimony again, and he kept it no secret. As for his oldest daughter, he was well pleased with her choice of Running Deer. He hoped one day in the near future they too would marry. As an added surprise, Evelyn's friend, Brenda, and her attorney, Greg Stuart, arrived together explaining that they were now betrothed.

Thomas and Evelyn were dressed in the style of the 1800s, as were many in the audience who were close friends and relatives.

As they stood in front of the altar of the old church, they joined together in the sacred ritual, saying their vows. Their happiness was reflected in a golden aura that surrounded them.

In the back of the church, lost among the crowd, a tall,

slightly overweight man with dark, wavy hair looked on with a melancholy expression that played upon his face. In his heart, he wanted only to wish them the best, yet he was envious and regretted his solitary state.

Once, he'd had wealth, a family of his own, and a woman he had loved but treated badly. Now he had nothing but the desire to prevent others from following in his footsteps. He reached in his pocket, took out his medication, turned, and walked out of the church.

Assured Evelyn and Bobby would be well taken care of, he would not bother them again.

It was best if they believed he had died in the terrible accident. He'd been badly injured, but with the help of a family from Okeechobee, he'd survived. With his hands in his pockets, his eyes cast down, he prayed God would forgive him for all of the harm he had done to others. Brakes screeched. James glanced up. Too late, he saw the car bearing down upon him.

Sirens sounded, faint at first, then louder. No one heard them except James and the man who had not stayed for the reception. Lying on the asphalt in front of St. Mary's Church, the last of his life force seeped from him. His vision blurred. Vince stood over him. He had always been there in his hour of need. But, when James saw the tunnel and the bright white light, he knew that no one could save him this time.

About the Author

Weslynn McCallister, pseudonym, Jamie Cortland was born in Evansville, Indiana and raised in Roswell, New Mexico. A published novelist and an award winning poet, she is a member of Sisters in Crime, the Mystery Writers of America, and is a founding member of the Florida Writers Association.

Educated in the fine arts, she has worked as a high fashion model, graphic designer, and as a real estate agent. Her hobby is ballroom dancing. Today, she lives in southwest Florida near the Gulf of Mexico.